Morning Glory Hill

Doris M. Dorwart

authorHOUSE®

AuthorHouse™
1663 Liberty Drive
Bloomington, IN 47403
www.authorhouse.com
Phone: 1 (800) 839-8640

Published by AuthorHouse   08/27/2016

ISBN: 978-1-5246-2670-9 (sc)
ISBN: 978-1-5246-2668-6 (hc)
ISBN: 978-1-5246-2669-3 (e)

Library of Congress Control Number: 2016914266

Print information available on the last page.

Acknowledgements

Having lived in an independent living facility for almost five years, I have had the opportunity to meet people who have had fabulous experiences as well as heart rendering tragedies. They have proven themselves to be thoughtful, kind, considerate friends and neighbors. They have come to accept their frailities. I hear the concern in their voices as they talk about a neighbor who is suffering in some manner. But hope for better days always seeps through their smiles and laughter. I thank them for all they do each day for one another to help make their paths just a little bit easier. As I watch them in the dining room and during various activities, my belief in their goodness only grows stronger.

My friends may see themselves in between the sentences of this book—favorite sayings, little habits, or maybe mode of dress. But I wondered what would happen if I could erase all their afflictions and replace them with fun, silliness, and romance, even for only a short period of time. So, out of my concern, and at the urging of Bernice Meyer, this little story was born. Don't worry about what it would cost to live at Morning Glory Hill, just enjoy what these quirky, lovable seniors do and say—laugh a little—and try to guess who inspired each character.

SPECIAL RECOGNITION

To the President of my Fan Club, Constance Soto, my *go-to-woman*, I owe a debt of gratitude. While we only have two members at this time, we hope that after this book circulates, our membership might swell to three or even four members.

Dedication

This book is dedicated to Joan Gast, a special lady that we lost all too soon. Remember, Joan, we *will* be friends forever. My life was made richer the day I met you. Thank you!

Chapter 1

The lights were beginning to bother Hortense. She wasn't sure if her discomfort was due to the heat of the lamps, or whether she was just nervous being interviewed by such a young reporter. She wished now that she had been smart enough to ask for a list of questions beforehand. The interview was being conducted in Morning Glory Square, the heart of the independent living facility she managed. She had worked hard to get this job and she was willing to do almost anything to hang on to it. Doing an interview was scary. Whatever she said would be captured forever on tape. In spite of having to compete with three men for the job, she had been chosen, so she decided to face this challenge head-on.

Her main goal was to make Morning Glory Hill an elegant, upper-class facility that would appeal to people of refinement and good taste. Although she felt that the leases to the apartments should have contained more restrictions on what the residents could not do, she didn't want to become a lady warden. However, keeping at bay any bad habits that residents might have was important to her. At the same time, she had to be careful how she dealt with issues when they arose. While she wanted to be friends with all the residents, she also had to conduct herself in such a manner that would always reconfirm the authority that she held.

To make it possible for the residents to participate in the interview, she had convened a panel of four. She chose only those she felt were more likely to make positive statements about their Morning Glory Hill experiences. The ladies, Marty Miller and Celeste Mayfair, had agreed immediately to join the panel. The two men, Samuel Long and Frank Snyder, had to be coaxed a bit. Her carefully hand-picked panel was ready.

Hortense scanned the room. All the sofas and lounge chairs in the room were occupied by other residents, who seemed to be thrilled to be part of the event. She could feel their eyes on her. Hortense knew she had to be careful in answering any questions posed by this young upstart from WDMD if she wanted to maintain her position of authority that meant so much to her.

"Good afternoon. I'm Chuck Cooper. Welcome to *What's New in the Community?* Today, I have the privilege of interviewing Hortense King, Director of Morning Glory Hill, an independent living facility that opened a little over a year ago. Miss King, would you please explain to our viewers what independent living is and how your mission addresses the needs of your residents?"

"Independent living is for men and women, sixty-five years and older, who no longer have the desire or the ability to live in their homes. For instance, they can no longer tolerate climbing stairs, or they do not have the physical ability to shovel snow, mow grass, or do the thousand other things that are involved in taking care of a home," Hortense explained. "Our mission is to make it possible for them to live in a safe environment that allows them the freedom to enjoy their lives, at their own pace, unburdened by worries of home ownership."

"I see. Now, Miss King, the other day when we talked on the phone you indicated that, from the air, Morning Glory Hill resembles an eight-pointed star. Can you expand on that, please?"

"Certainly," Hortense replied, using her most authoritative voice. "However, first let me say that we owe a debt of gratitude to Mr. and Mrs. Amos Smoker, who not only provided the land on which this remarkable building stands, but they financed the entire project. Mrs. Smoker insisted on providing first-floor apartments for everyone to ensure easy access. Six wings, or as we call them, *lanes*, hold apartments for the residents and the other two are for restaurants, a gift shop, a swimming pool, and other such services. She further directed that each lane be named after a flower."

Chuck turned to the panel. "I would like to ask you a few questions about Morning Glory Hill," he said as Hortense held her breath. "Hortense has requested that I use your first names. Marty, what do you like most about Morning Glory Hill?"

"That's an easy one to answer—the other residents. I was surprised when I grew so old so early. So, the pain was eased by making so many new friends," Marty said as she gestured towards the residents sitting nearby. I appreciate having access to Hannah's Mediation Room where we can find peace. Oh, and the spa is one of my favorites—one refreshes the body, the other the soul."

"Celeste, how do you occupy your day at Morning Glory Hill?" Chuck asked.

"I act as the librarian. I make sure that everyone gets the kind of reading materials they enjoy," Celeste said proudly. pointing to her little red wagon filled with books.

With a little smile on his face, Chuck asked coyly, "Any kind of reading materials?"

Celeste sat up straight. "Yes, you heard right. However, our library does have a collection development policy. So, some things are off limits due to budgetary concerns. Remember, young man, your generation did not invent salacious materials."

"Oh, Celeste, you must be a remarkable librarian," Chuck teased. "Now, Samuel, what do you like about living here?" Chuck said as the crowd quieted down.

"First and foremost, Oscar can live with me. And, before you ask, Oscar is my cat." Samuel said a bit on the curt side.

"Oh, a man with a cat. That's a bit unusual, isn't it?"

"I don't see anything unusual about that at all!" Samuel stated firmly.

Cooper quickly moved on. "Frank, how about you? What's your take on Morning Glory Hill?"

"I have to agree with Marty. The people here are thoughtful and considerate of one another. You don't normally find that in a regular apartment house," Frank said.

"How about the cost?" the reporter quizzed.

"I'm so old that I remember when water was free. Nothing's free anymore," Frank replied. "Before you leave, take a look at *Hannah's Meditation Room.* My only regret is that I believe old age comes at a really bad time."

Cooper couldn't help but smile at this remark. "Folks, thank you so much for participating in this little interview. Just one more question for you, Hortense: Are your residents involved in technology in any way?"

"Of course. Right next to our library, we have a fully equipped computer room," Hortense said proudly.

"I would have thought that seniors wouldn't be comfortable with new, intrusive electronic devices," Cooper said as he looked over the crowd.

"Mr. Cooper, while our residents are all over sixty-five, they are not dead yet," Hortense said dramatically.

Some of the residents stood up and applauded. Cooper was taken back and looked very sheepish. While Hortense tried to hide the fact that she was smiling, she was delighted that she had given that fresh young reporter a taste of her displeasure.

"Miss King, I meant no disrespect. But I am amazed at what is going on in Morning Glory Hill. You have so many options for the residents."

"Tell me, Mr. Cooper, where can you find a place that offers any more services than what we have here at Morning Glory Hill?"

A voice from the crowd, shouted, "Tell him about *The Night Owl*."

As the residents laughed and clapped their hands, Hortense actually giggled. "That's a small area near our *Sassy Cat Café* that has a counter and two tables and chairs where residents can go between 10 p.m. and 6 a.m. to get a bite to eat when the late night *hungries* strike. Our residents sometimes show up wearing their night clothes and they love the informality of *The Night Owl*."

Cooper leaned back in his chair and laughed along with the residents. "Oh, Miss King, this is really an amazing place," he said as he wiped the tears from his cheeks. "Are you at liberty to tell us what it costs to rent an apartment here?"

"No, and there's a reason for that. We have various-sized apartments. However, they all come with large living rooms, a fully-equipped kitchen, a bedroom with a walk-in closet, a den, a laundry area, and, of course, a bathroom with a step-in shower as well as a whirlpool tub. Grab bars are conveniently placed as well as emergency pull cords that residents can use when they need assistance. Some people require more floor space than others. But, all apartments accommodate wheelchairs. They also have a plethora of amenities to choose from."

"Can you give us a sample of the amenities?"

"They run from the simple things such as newspapers and cable service, all the way to standing spa or beauty shop appointments, to transportation anywhere in the county. Each apartment comes with one underground parking space. Residents may dine at any of our food areas, or have room service delivery and charge it to their accounts. So you see, it is entirely up to the residents just how many services they want or need."

"I'm ready to move in right now," Cooper said.

Hortense laughed. "Well, young man, see me when you are a bit older."

Just then, Hortense spotted Ellie May Dunkel, hurrying across The Square, frantically waving her hands in the air, Sensing there was a problem, Hortense whispered to Cooper that he should end his Q and A session and bring the interview to an end. "When will this be aired?" she asked the reporter.

"Probably during the noon broadcast tomorrow. Thank you, Miss King, you were very generous with your time," Cooper said as he began to help his cameraman gather the electric cords.

Hortense moved over to Ellie May and pulled her to the side. "What's wrong?"

"It's Nigel again," she replied as she tugged on the straps of her white apron.

"Oh, no. What is it this time?"

"He's running up and down Daffodil Lane without any trousers on," a mortified Ellie May said. "And, he's wearing black silk boxer shorts that have red ants all over."

"Not real ones?" Hortense asked as she raised her eyebrows.

"No, I mean pictures of ants. It's totally disgusting."

"Is he exposed in any way?" Hortense asked cautiously.

"Heavens, I don't know. I didn't look," Ellie May replied as she blushed.

Hortense and Ellie May practically flew across The Square to Daffodil Lane. Hortense had to be careful with this incident. After all, the residents were supposed to be independent, but she still had the responsibility for maintaining a high level of decorum.

William Williams was standing in the hallway, laughing and holding his sides, while Nigel Nuggett was galloping down the hallway in his underwear, waving his arms in the air. "William," Hortense called out, "for heaven's sake, what is going on here?"

"Nothing much," William replied. "I bet Nigel a free lunch that he was too chicken to run down the hall with just those wild boxer shorts on. He proved me wrong," William said between fits of laughter. "Don't worry. All our women folk are okay," he said as he pushed a well-worn Stetson hat back a bit further on his head.

Nigel halted in front of Hortense and William with a broad smile on his face. "Don't ever tell me that I'm too chicken to do anything, William. My daily horoscope told me that I was in for some fun today. See, William, it was right again," he said as his chubby cheeks seemed to jump up and down with every word. "Now, I think it's time for you to buy me lunch."

Hortense had heard a rumor that Nigel sometimes drank whiskey out of a thermos bottle, but she had no proof of such behavior. "William, why do you egg him on to do silly things like this? Some residents may not appreciate your sense of humor."

William sighed and adjusted his hat. "Hortense, let me tell you something—if some of these ladies would relax a bit, and stop being so straight-laced, they just might feel better. Nigel didn't offend anyone."

Hortense got a good look at Nigel's shorts. Personally, she thought they were ugly. She couldn't imagine why anyone would even want to wear ants on their underpants. Suddenly, she felt itchy all over.

Chapter 2

"Rosebud, you just did what?" Marty asked.

"I had the maintenance man put another shoe rack in my closet," Rosebud said proudly.

"Rosebud, you already have two shoe racks. You surely don't need another one."

"Marty, you know that I love, love shoes and more shoes. I know it's an addiction, but I love shoes—all kinds. What does it hurt if I do?" Rosebud asked.

"Well, I guess you're right, Imelda Marcus. And, it's really none of my business if you have a hundred pairs of shoes."

"I don't have a hundred pairs—only 83," Rosebud replied thoughtfully. "Anyway, I have a question for you. How about your doll collection? I bet you have 100 dolls or more. And, some of them you keep under lock and key. At least I can wear my addiction! Now, sit down and have a cup of coffee with me. My sister brought me some homemade sticky buns last night. I'll pop them in the microwave."

"Sounds good to me," Marty said. "Did you hear about the ruckus on Daffodil yesterday?"

"No, what happened?"

"Nigel ran up and down the hallway without his trousers on," Marty said as she laughed.

"That had to be a sight that would give one heart palpations," a wide-eyed Rosebud said dryly.

"Abigail is all uptight about it," Marty said.

"Why does she care? She lives on Marigold. That old biddy should keep her nose out of other people's business," Rosebud said as she took a sip of coffee. "I make a good cup of coffee, don't I?"

"Rosebud, you use a Keurig—it *makes* the coffee," Marty patiently reminded her friend.

"I have to put the water in and the little thing-ama-jig of coffee," Rosebud argued. "Marty, I just want you to know that I really love your doll collection. They probably bring back many happy childhood memories for you."

"I never had a doll when I was young," Marty said quietly. "On our wedding day, Charlie presented me with a bride doll—they were all the rage back then. In her hands, Charlie had placed sparkling crystal earrings for me. He never demonstrated such creativity before. I was taken back. I made such a fuss over that doll that he just kept them coming. When I look at my dolls, I see and hear my Charlie and I feel happy and content. That's silly, I know," Marty said.

"How do you decide which dolls you want to add to your collection?" Rosebud asked.

"I get several catalogs and I also surf the Internet. I sometimes feel like a junkie," Marty said as she laughed. "I really like my bride dolls the best. For instance, there's a new bride doll listed on the Bradford Exchange for around two hundred. I think I'll get it. It's a twenty-one inch doll that is absolutely beautiful. Most of my dolls did not cost that much. Most were in the twenty to fifty dollar range. My Aunt Marty, who never married, kept a doll on her bed that, as a child, I thought was the prettiest doll in the world. I don't know what ever happened to that doll, but I wish I had her in my collection. To make certain that my dolls live on, I have willed them all to my great granddaughter. Every time Gretchen visits me, we sit on my bed and have fun with the dolls."

"But what about that doll you mentioned one time—googly eyed or something like that? Isn't that one valuable?"

"She is an antique Googly-eyed, all bisque doll with a smiling face. Charlie got that one for me right after we were married. Just recently, I discovered that she is now worth over ten thousand dollars," Marty confided.

"You're kidding! Ten thousand dollars for a doll?" Rosebud responded.

"Well, you know, I always say there's no accounting for what people will pay for things. Just like my aunt's old doll—if she would be listed for sale, regardless of the price, I would buy her."

Marty wanted to tell Rosebud about the necklace she had discovered, but she was afraid. That morning, she had decided to clean out the wardrobe where Charlie used to keep his clothes. She found his old Dopp kit and almost tossed it in the trash. But, as she took it in her hands, she felt something in the bottom. Pulling back the lining of the bag, she saw a glittering necklace of diamonds. She wasn't certain that the jewels were real. Since her husband used to travel with some strange people—whom she had always suspected were criminals, she also didn't want her husband's legacy to be besmirched. While Charlie had made a good income selling used cars, she was sure that he could not have afforded to buy a real diamond necklace. She was certain that Rosebud would know if they were real diamonds since she and her husband had owned a jewelry store for years. But, could she really tell anyone? Suddenly, Marty realized that she had drifted off and Rosebud was talking to her.

"Marty, are you listening? I'm going to tell you something that I've never told anyone. When I was a little girl, we were so poor that when I got a hole in the sole of my shoe, my dad would line my shoe with cardboard. So here we are—two grown women, still fighting off unpleasant memories from the Depression."

The women grew silent. They were both lost, recalling long-held memories. The only sound that could be heard was the ticking of a clock. They jumped when the doorbell rang.

"Come in," Rosebud called out.

"Hello, ladies," Ellie May replied as she eyed the sticky buns. "Sorry I'm late, but I was watching an episode of *True Detective* and I had to see how it ended."

"You and your crime stories. Maybe you should consider becoming a detective," Marty teased.

"Your timing is right on target," Rosebud said as she jumped up to put another bun in the microwave.

The three women had formed a bond almost as soon as they had met. Even though they were vastly different from one another, they spent most of their days doing things as a group. Marty was a woman who had always paid attention to fashion. She could recite what the 'in-thing' was for almost any given year. She subscribed to four fashion magazines and would spend considerable time perusing them from cover to cover. Ellie May, on the other hand, dressed like a housewife from the 50s—flowered dresses, white aprons, and orthopedic shoes. She refused to wear slacks. Rosebud, however, was the most outlandish—fishnet stockings, miniskirts, high heels, and bright red nail polish—and she never went anywhere without first applying her makeup. But, somehow, all these differences were overlooked—the women simply liked one another.

"These buns are delicious—almost as good as the ones I make," Ellie May teased.

"But you are a kitchen genius," Rosebud said. "You ought to go on TV. You know, one of those shows where they have baking contests. You'd win hands down."

"Did I tell you there's a new couple moving in today on Lilac? I'll be visiting them later on to give them their Morning Glory Hill gift basket. They're next to the Hamiltons. I hope they get along with Harvey and Harry—they are such a nice couple. The only one here who still doesn't accept them is Abigail," Marty said.

"I cannot believe Abigail's parents chose that name for her. If I'm not mistaken, Abigail means *joy of the father*. The only way she could be a joy would be if she would stop criticizing everyone and everything," Ellie May sniffed as she lightly pounded the table.

"Ellie May, you're too much," Rosebud said.

"Have things quieted down over Nigel's prank?" Marty asked as she took the last bite of her bun.

"It upset me at first," Ellie May said. "But after I had time to think about it, I wrote it off to Nigel's weird sense of humor. But I heard that Abigail plans to submit a formal complaint to the Mayors Board."

"But she lives on Marigold," Marty said incredulously.

"We all know that she's a little peculiar. Unless she's talking about her piles of money, or someone else's business, she's not happy," Rosebud said. "It was a sorry day when she moved into this place. She doesn't get it. Maybe she's so unhappy that she wants to make us all that way. We have such little time left. Could we get her evicted somehow? Hey, maybe we could get her hooked up with Nigel—thoughts? Oh, my, now I'm beginning to sound like her," Rosebud said as she put her hand over her mouth.

"She'll never run out of money. We hear all the time that she only buys the best. Maybe we could start a rumor about her. Maybe she does need a man," Marty said as she giggled.

"Even Nigel has better taste than that," Rosebud said forlornly.

"When I lived in Florida, we had a lady like Abigail. We set her up with a traveling salesman and they ran off together," Marty said excitedly.

"Do either of you know any available traveling salesmen?" Rosebud teased.

"What about William Willams? He's available," Ellie May suggested.

"He's not her type," Marty argued.

"We won't know until we try. William is my neighbor. He plays the piano and has a nice voice. I know he dresses like a cowboy, but he's a nice person," Ellie May said convincingly.

Rosebud clapped her hands together. "It just might work. Even if we can't get her to move, maybe William could take that sneer off her face and replace it with a smile. You know, I think we are on to something here. There's nothing we can't accomplish if we work together. Okay, let's call this *Operation Smile*. Ellie May, you start the ball rolling by dropping hints to William about Abigail. I'll do the same."

"I've got it," Marty said excitedly. "How about we have an elegant tea? We could ask Abigail to sing and William to play. This means they would have to get together to practice. Oh, and we could make it more special by making it an annual event…something the women could look forward to. We can all wear hats and garden-type dresses—oh, it will be so much fun."

"I love it," Rosebud said. "I was on *The Queen Mary* one time and I went to a high tea."

"What's the difference between an elegant tea and a high tea?" Ellie May asked.

"High tea is usually served between 7 and 9 p.m. and includes a meat dish of some kind. An elegant tea is usually served at 4 o'clock and includes small sandwiches, scones, and little cakes served with jam and butter," Rosebud explained. "Our tea should include beautiful china, pretty teapots, folded napkins, and doilies. You know—real girly—pretty tablecloths and flowers."

"I'll ask Abigail to sing," Marty added. "Rosebud, you ask William to play. That should help us a lot."

"What's the date?" Rosebud asked.

"Check with William. We can make it almost any day that he's available. Rosebud, you get a date," Marty instructed.

"I hope you don't mean a date—date. I think you mean a date that he can play. Can you imagine me dating William?" Rosebud asked as they all giggled in unison.

The women agreed to meet in the dining room for dinner at 6. As soon as Marty closed her apartment door behind her, her thoughts went back to the necklace. When she reached into the well-worn Dopp kit to retrieve the necklace, Charlie crossed her mind. Oh, how she had loved that man. While Charlie was a little rough around the edges, he was a good man. They had two sons; unfortunately one died when he was only eight years old.

Gently, she removed the necklace from its hiding place and laid it over her bride doll. She thought it looked amazing—the bride was enveloped in diamonds—what bride wouldn't want to look like that? She tried counting the diamonds. Lovingly, she draped the necklace over her hands. The three strands of gems sparkled in an enticing manner. In the center of each strand were several beautiful garnets that grew larger with each strand. Marty had never seen a necklace so beautiful. Softly, she whispered, "Charlie, my precious Charlie, help me with this. What should I do? I could always depend on you to take care of me."

Chapter 3

It was Rosebud's turn to get involved in *Operation Smile*. She headed to Daffodil Lane, all the while going over in her head what she needed to say to the piano player. She was pleased that her legs felt so good today since she was able to leave her jeweled cane at home. She really loved that cane, but somehow she always felt younger when she didn't need it.

When she reached William's apartment, she could hear him playing. Ellie May often talked about how much she enjoyed his music and was pleased that she was his neighbor. Rosebud wished that Ellie May were with her now to give her the confidence that she was going to need to pull this off. She had taken extreme care in getting dressed this morning. While she loved her fishnet stockings, she decided that she needed to bring it down a notch since she was on a mission. Rosebud thought that her conservative skirt and blouse would help to bolster her efforts to be professional. After all, if *Operation Smile* were successful, Abigail would be happier and then perhaps the entire population of Morning Glory Hill would be, too. She pressed the doorbell.

As the door opened, Rosebud was surprised when she saw that William was in a bathrobe. "Why, Rosebud, hello. What a nice surprise," William said happily.

"I came to ask you for a favor, William," Rosebud said a little nervously. The bathrobe really increased her apprehension.

"Well, come on in," William said as he held the door open wide. "It isn't often that I get lady callers," the pianist said as he smiled at Rosebud.

Rosebud wasn't sure that it would be proper for her to go into the apartment considering the manner in which William was dressed. But, bravely, she decided that she would be safe. After all, Ellie May was right next door in case she had to be rescued.

"What a charming piano," Rosebud said shyly, not certain how she was going to lead the conversation to Abigail.

"I bought that when I decided to move here. The one I had before would have been too large for this room. Since then, however, I've regretted not bringing it along since we could have used it in so many other places here at Morning Glory. Well, so much for Monday morning quarterbacking," William said as he scurried around the room picking up sheet music. "Rosebud, make yourself comfortable," he said as he nervously tried to tidy up. "You said you had a favor to ask. Now, tell me. How can I help such a fashionable lady?"

Rosebud could feel herself blushing. "We're planning a tea next month for the ladies, and Marty appointed me to see if you would consider playing for us. Well, to be honest, it was really Abigail's idea. She said you play like a professional."

"That's quite a compliment. I do play for various organizations, but not on a regular basis. However, I would be delighted to play for the ladies' tea. Rosebud, will you please excuse me for a few minutes? I just realized that I am still in my bathrobe."

"Of course, William."

Rosebud sauntered around the living room that she judged to be posh western. She examined a beautiful Baldwin coffee table that was positioned in front of a Zelmo sofa, framed with end tables that held Bradbury lamps. On the other side of the room was a a light blue Corncome club chair right next to the piano. Rosebud was familiar with these pieces since her brother had had his home decorated from top to bottom in western style. She was impressed when she realized that William also had interesting western prints on the wall—one by Alfred Miller and several others by Charles Russell. She couldn't wait to tell Marty that William Williams was much more than just a want-to-be cowboy.

As William came back into the room, he asked. "Do you have a date for the tea?"

"We were thinking about the 15th, but we're willing to change that if you're already booked for that day," Rosebud said.

"That date is fine with me. What kind of music would you like? You know, country western is my favorite, but somehow I don't think that would be appropriate for your tea," William said as he chuckled.

"I must confess, I'm not really familiar with country western. Is that like the songs that Garth Brooks sings?"

"You bettcha. Brooks happens to lead all others in country western sales. Would you believe that he's sold over 125 million albums? He's set the standard. Others in the field may never top his record," William explained.

Rosebud opened her eyes wide and smiled at William. "I had no idea! I used to think that country western meant those songs the cowboys would sing as they rode the range. You know, like the ones in the movies with Roy Rogers and Tom Mix," she said as she giggled.

"You're close, Rosebud. That kind of music was considered 'folk' music and was considered degrading by many in the music business. But, in the 40s, things began to change and country western, as we know it today, was born."

"Oh," Rosebud said excitedly, "I know what—your music would be ideal for our August barbeque! Would you consider that, too?"

"Sure would. But we need to settle on music for the tea. How about elevator music? You know—soft music, soothing songs, love songs and such."

"Oh, William, you are fantastic. When I was discussing the tea the other day with Abigail, she suggested music from the 40s and 50s. You know, she's quite interested in music. Another idea just popped into my head—Abigail has an exquisite voice and perhaps the two of you could perform together. What do you think? You're the expert," Rosebud said coyly.

"Thank you, Rosebud, but I'm surely not an expert. If Abigail wants to sing, and she's comfortable with me, then I say, let's go in that direction."

"I know that she has performed professionally and she also sings at her church. Oh, and another thing—Abigail mentioned to me that she used to take piano lessons and she would like to try taking lessons again. Would you be interested in teaching?" Rosebud asked politely.

"I'm not sure about that. Let me think about it. But, you can definitely count on me for the 15th of next month. Just tell Abigail that anytime she's ready to choose her music, she should give me a buzz and I'll be happy to accompany her."

On the way out the door, Rosebud stopped and shook William's hand. "One more thing about Abigail that you probably don't know. She funds a program at Smoker Elementary for students who cannot afford to purchase instruments to play in the school band. She's such a thoughtful lady. Don't you agree?" Rosebud asked as she finally removed her hand from William's grip.

As William closed the door behind him, he broke out in a big smile. When he first established residency at Morning Glory Hill, he had thought that he would not be interested in any women. After all, his track record with four failed marriages spoke for itself. He was just not *husband* material. But, perhaps here, with so many new friends, he shouldn't squander the chance to turn his life around.

He dug his cell phone out of his pocket and called Nigel. "Nigel, guess what. I think I have an admirer here at Morning Glory Hill… certainly it's a woman…of course, I know I was married and divorced four times…oh, you want to know who it is…why, it's Rosebud."

Chapter 4

"Rosebud, we're dying to hear how it went when you visited William," Ellie May said eagerly as she looked over the menu in *The Sassy Cat Café*. "I almost knocked on William's door to find out, but I thought that might not be a good idea in case it went badly."

"Oh yes, I want to hear all about it," Marty said as she moved her wrought iron chair closer to the table.

"Can't right now," Rosebud whispered. "Here comes Abigail."

"As I was saying," Marty said, "I ordered my shoes from *Foot Smart*—a bit pricey for me, but they were just what I was looking for to go with my new long skirt. Rosebud, you're the shoe expert. What do you think?"

"I should get a pair like that," Rosebud mused.

"Wait a minute, your shoe trees are filled," Ellie May teased. "Good morning, Abigail. Won't you join us? We're going to have some ice cream and sit out on the patio just to enjoy this early spring day."

"I'll sit down a bit, but I don't want any ice cream. It would spoil my dinner," Abigail said gruffly. "Marty, your hair looks a bit whiter today. Did you have something done?"

"Nothing new—it's my own hair—no color—and it's my same style," Marty replied in a rapid fire manner.

"I used to wear my hair that way," Abigail said, "but, *that* was way back when I was in high school. It's just not seen as stylish anymore."

"I'll let you borrow my latest fashion magazine, Abigail. Right on the cover of *Elle* is a model with this same hair style. Perhaps that just got by you," Marty said as she turned on the charm.

Abigail shrugged her shoulders and turned to Ellie May. "I saw you walking your dog yesterday. She's put on a few pounds lately, wouldn't you say?"

Stuttering, Ellie May replied, "Why... no... I don't think so. I had her to the vet last week and he thinks she's just the right weight."

Rosebud thought she'd better jump into this conversation before any more insults flew. "Abigail, William has agreed to play for the ladies' tea and he said all you have to do is call him to arrange your practice time. He's looking forward to hearing you sing," Rosebud said kindly.

"Ordinarily, William would not have been my choice to serve as my accompanist. But I guess he's the best we can do," Abigail said with a sigh, "I hope he doesn't make me look bad."

Ellie May was glaring at Abigail, but she didn't seem to notice. "Abigail, William is an accomplished musician and he has played for many events and for lots of people. He has agreed to let you choose the songs you want to sing. I think the residents will be surprised to hear the two of you since you're both professional musicians." As Abigail changed the expression on her face, Ellie May said evenly, "William is my neighbor and a finer gentleman I have never met."

"You have more faith in some of these people who live here than I do. Many of them have no class at all. Especially that silly Jessie who always rhymes whatever she hears with the most inane things that seem to pop into her empty head. I doubt that many residents here have had any advanced education as far as the fine arts are concerned. But, I'm willing to help by participating in the entertainment for the tea. I must run along now. I have a standing spa appointment. I'll call William later," Abigail said as she walked away.

They watched as Abigail strutted back into the building on her way to the spa. "Good grief, Charlie Brown, did anyone count the number of insults that she laid on us during the few minutes that she was here?" Marty asked. "She really gets under my skin. I wanted to knock her on her ass."

"Marty." Ellie May said. "Just let the insults run off your shoulder. I didn't like the way she talked about my Sophie. I love that dog and she's not getting fat."

"I hope she doesn't insult William that way. He may back out of playing all together," Rosebud said. "But, remember *Operation Smile*. We're not sure what will come out of our efforts to pair those two, but let's not give up too soon. We may be doing mankind a favor if we can turn Abigail around. You know, she's not a bad-looking woman when she smiles, but unfortunately she doesn't do that very often. For her age, she's got a nice figure and her wire-rimmed glasses look good on her. She just seems to have a large chip on her shoulder. Too bad...too bad."

"Ladies, are you ready to order," the server from the cafe asked.

"Make it three hot fudge sundaes with gobs of whipped cream," Rosebud said. "We need a *pick-me-up*."

"Even that old biddy I knew in Florida—you know, the one who ran away with the traveling salesman—was not as mean as Abigail. I bet if she met the Lord Himself she would find something wrong with Him in two seconds."

Just as the server placed the sundaes in front of them, Marty turned to Rosebud and said, "I was watching a film the other day and the host mentioned imitation diamonds. My curiosity was piqued and I was wondering: How does one tell the difference between diamonds that are real from those that are made by man?"

"You can put the diamond in front of your mouth and fog it as if it were a mirror. If it stays fogged for a couple of seconds, it's probably a fake. If the setting is of poor quality, then it's probably a fake. Visually, it's almost impossible to tell a man-made diamond from a mined diamond. Using a jeweler's loupe can also be helpful. But it's best to have a jeweler examine it," Rosebud explained. "Some jewelers also use cultured rubies, emeralds and sapphires. When we had our shop, I remember a customer who had promised his wife a diamond necklace for their twenty-fifth wedding anniversary, but he didn't have the money. So, for less than ten percent of what a real diamond necklace would have cost, he had a cultured one made. I had the opportunity to examine it and the stones had almost the same clarity and color as real diamonds."

"Did the wife ever find out that her necklace was not real?" Ellie May asked.

"Good question, but I don't know the answer," Rosebud giggled.

Marty now felt a lot better. She didn't want to believe that her husband had been involved in any shady deals. So, she decided that the necklace she had found was phony. But, if she ever found the courage, she would show it to Rosebud anyway and find out for certain. Real or not, that necklace was an unusual piece.

Charlie never showed her his paycheck. She had no idea how much he had earned. But he managed to send their son to college and Marty herself never wanted for a thing. Whenever she had been tempted to ask him about some of his friends, she would recall that her mother had warned her about asking questions that she really didn't want to know the answer and this was just such a question. Then again, it was kind of exhilarating to think that maybe Charlie had been connected to the mob. That would make her his moll. She had to smile at the very thought of such a thing. Ellie May would love it!

Chapter 5

It was the second Tuesday of the month, so it was time for the Morning Glory Hill Mayors Council meeting. The president of the Council, Samuel Long, was the first to arrive at the meeting room. After he adjusted the blinds, he began placing the name plates for the other five mayors on the table. He was a firm believer that when everything was in its proper place, the meeting would be successful.

He opened his iPad and tapped a few keys. Then he sat back to look over what he had just entered. His book, a tell-all manuscript about Morning Glory Hill, was coming along nicely. He estimated that he had been completing about three or four pages each day. Samuel viewed his neighbors with disdain. They all thought they were superior to him. The women were particularly galling. A confirmed bachelor, Samuel tried to keep his distance from the ladies. He especially didn't like that Abigail woman and he hoped that she wouldn't show up for today's meeting. To make matters even more uncomfortable, Marty had requested help with some kind of tea. He had a difficult time dealing with any of these silly female activities. He didn't know anything about teas, and he didn't want to know—he had other things on his mind.

He smiled as he remembered a little ditty that he used to sing to his pesky little sister. He closed his eyes and quietly began to mumble: *Rachel, Rachel, I've been thinking/What a great world this would be/If the girls were all transported/Far across the big blue sea.*

It didn't surprise him that Sally, Mayor of Marigold Lane, was the first to arrive. No matter what was happening, she always had to be first. He didn't like her at all, but he smiled and said, "Good morning." He felt that the least the uncouth woman could have done was to recognize his greeting.

His thoughts were interrupted when Ellie May, Mayor of Daffodil Lane, and Marty, Mayor of Lilac Lane, entered the room. "Good morning, ladies. Here are your packets of information for today's meeting. No serious topics today, but we do have several events to plan."

"Samuel, I admire your organization abilities. You need to give me some pointers on organizing my paperwork. Each year at tax time, I tell myself that I'll be organized next year, but, somehow, next year comes and my desk is still a mess," Marty said. "However, I do take good care of my doll collection and I can proudly say that they are well organized."

"That means you prize your collection, Marty. Don't fret about your paper work; just give all your receipts to your accountant and let him worry about it," Samuel said pretentiously.

The last two mayors arrived together. Frank Snyder, Mayor of Orchid Lane, and Celeste Mayfair, Mayor of Petunia Lane, picked up their packets, greeted everyone and joined the others at the head table. Residents began arriving, and at precisely ten, Samuel rapped his gavel and brought the meeting to order. He was disappointed when he spied Abigail taking a seat. While he held a Doctorate in Education, he felt woefully unprepared to deal with the whining, complaining Abigail.

The discussions were moving along smoothly and Samuel was holding out hope that perhaps Abigail would not cause any problems today since he was almost at the end of his agenda. His contentment, however, was short-lived when Abigail stood up.

"Yes, Abigail," the board president said.

"The other day there was an incident on Daffodil Lane. A half-naked man ran up and down the hallway minus his trousers. What do you intend to do about this unacceptable behavior?" Abigail said as she sat down again.

Nigel, who was sitting in the last row, hunched down in his seat. He wanted to say something to that old biddy, but then he reconsidered and decided to remain quiet.

"Samuel, may I please take this?" Marty asked. She waited until she saw Samuel nod his head and then she stood up. "Let me assure all of you, the man was not half-naked. Granted, he did not have his trousers on, but he was wearing boxer shorts. This all happened as a result of a silly, little bet made between two residents. It was over in a matter of a few minutes. No one on Daffodil Lane has complained. In fact, they felt that it brought a little levity into their lives," Marty said as she laughed.

Abigail jumped out of her seat. "I see nothing funny about *that* incident. It should never have happened. Perhaps he'll be completely naked the next time," Abigail said indignantly as she sat down and crossed her arms.

Barry Adams, Activities Director of Morning Glory Hill, stood up. "I realize that I'm only a guest, Samuel, but do I have your permission to address this issue."

"Of course, Barry, go ahead."

"I have spoken with the two residents involved in this little incident, and they have promised not to pull any more pranks such as the one we are discussing. They were just having a bit of fun," Barry said as he adjusted his navy blue blazer emblazoned with large gold buttons. His blonde hair was combed straight back from his face and he made an impressive appearance. A former activities director for a cruise line, Barry always looked like he was ready to step right back into his previous job. Looking directly at Abigail, Barry said, "By the way, Abigail, I heard some exciting news last evening. I understand that we're going to have the unique privilege of hearing you sing at the ladies' tea. I'll be the emcee for that event and I'm looking forward to your presentation."

Abigail immediately changed the expression on her face. "Thank you, Barry. I can always depend on you for demonstrating good manners."

"I understand that Harvey has an announcement to make," Samuel said.

"As most of you know, I am a devoted Phillies fan. Through some of my contacts, I can get thirty senior citizen tickets for an afternoon game sometime during the month of June. I'll give the information to Celeste for our newsletter. Since I played Double-A ball for two seasons, I simply cannot get enough of baseball. So let's make it a fun day at the ball park," Harvey said enthusiastically. "Also, please stop by our apartment on Friday afternoon around four. Harry and I are giving our new neighbors, Gordon and Marie Turnbull, a little wine and cheese welcome party. They are a delightful couple. I'll be sure to put a little notice on the bulletin board, but I thought I would give you a heads-up on the party."

"Thanks, Harvey," Samuel said. "You can put me down for one of those seats for the ball game. I'll also be delighted to stop by your party. How nice of you to welcome your neighbors in such a manner. Marty, I understand you have an announcement to make."

"As Barry mentioned, there will be an elegant tea held in our dining room on the 15th of next month. You'll learn more about this fabulous activity in the newsletter you will be receiving tomorrow. While we already have a committee working on getting all the fineries that will be required, we really need two men to volunteer to help on that day," Marty explained.

"I'm willing to help with the setup," Frank said. "If you need someone to hang things up, I can do that, too, but I'm not good at decorating." He watched Marty intently. She certainly was a fine-looking woman.

Nigel sheepishly put his hand up. "Marty, I can help, too, if you would like. I really want to hear William and Abigail perform."

"Great," Marty said. "I'll call to let you know what time we'll be setting up. Gentlemen, the ladies thank you."

"Anything else?" Samuel asked.

Barry raised his hand. "It has come to my attention that there is some confusion regarding how groups are assigned to common areas, particularly meeting rooms. I believe that we have worked that out and, hopefully, that won't happen again. However, if it does, please report that to me." Barry suddenly felt that he was back on the cruise ship—people looking for rooms, not knowing aft from stern, and simply not following directions. He smiled as he pictured the residents wearing life vests, standing at attention, while he reviewed safety procedures at the muster stations.

"Thanks, Barry. Is there any other business to come before the Board?"

Jessie, who had been sitting very quietly in the back row, stood up, banged her cane on the floor, and said, *"I heard a lot today, but I have something more to say, I'll be hurrying on my way, to see more naked men today,"* she said with a sly smile.

The meeting ended in a burst of laughter.

Chapter 6

Marty was busy preparing Room B for her monthly book club meeting. It was also her turn to present background information on Nora Roberts, their featured author of the month. Each club member had been instructed to read one of Roberts' books and to prepare some thoughts about it at the meeting. It probably had been difficult for the members to choose just one book since Roberts had written more than 200 romance novels. Of course, they could also choose one of the books from her 'death' series that she wrote under the pen name of J.D. Robb. Marty had made a mental note to ask Abigail to remain when the meeting was over, since she was ready to do her part to make *Operation Smile* a success.

Rosebud came bursting into the room in her usual dramatic fashion. "Wow, I'm the first to arrive," she said as she took the seat beside Marty. "Oh, before the others arrive, I have to tell you an 'Abigail' story. Well, I'm sitting in The Square with Celeste when Abigail comes over and, lo and behold, she sits down next to Celeste. Celeste had been showing me some photographs of her son and his children—wait till you hear this part—you won't believe this—Abigail looks at the photo and remarks, 'What a good-looking group of teenagers.' Then—this is the best part— well then she says,—'Are they by chance adopted?'"

"She didn't say that, did she?" Marty asked incredulously.

"She sure did. Well—you should have seen Celeste's face—she was livid and she replied, 'What do you mean by that insult?' Then Abigail says, 'I don't know what you mean *my insult*—I just asked a question!' So then Celeste grabs her photos and says, 'You are a mean, spiteful, dried-up, old woman' and storms off. It could mean fireworks in here today if they both show up. You better be on your guard," Rosebud cautioned.

"I'm glad you filled me in. I don't think that Celeste will say anything about the incident but I'm not too certain that Abigail will let it go," Marty said just as other club members arrived.

Copies of Roberts' books were being placed on the table. Celeste said, "This certainly looks like a wonderful tribute to Nora."

"Oh, you're on a first name basis with the author?" Jessie teased.

"Certainly. I've read so many of her books that I really feel like a friend."

"Won't you be my friend, before my life comes to an end?" Jessie teased.

Marty began her meeting promptly at two. "Welcome, everyone. Today is Nora Roberts Day. Since it was my turn to research the author, I'll begin my brief report on this amazingly talented woman. Sometimes we take the author of a book for granted, especially if we have read the author's work before. We read the book—enjoy it—but we seldom wonder how a particular book came to be."

"You know, Marty, I never thought of that until we started doing research on authors. I myself have since developed a new appreciation for the work that goes into a book," Celeste said. "Or, does anyone think that knowing more about the author will get in the way of truly enjoying a story as it unfolds?"

Jesse raised her hand and said, "I think knowing a bit about the author of any given book could deepen our appreciation of the finished product. When I look over the shelves at the bookstore, and I see the number of books written by a particular author, I sometimes wonder how one person can keep generating stories that are unique and interesting. Or, should we just enjoy the story and not over-analyze how it came to be?"

"But, some authors are 'one-book' wonders. Not that their one book wasn't great, but then look at *To Kill a Mockingbird*—we waited and waited and we were rewarded with *Go Set a Watchman*. Then there are other authors who keep on churning them out," Rosebud said.

"Well, let's take a more in-depth look at Nora Roberts," Marty said. "Before she became an author, she was housebound with her two young sons during a blizzard in 1979. According to my research, this experience generated a love of the writing process in her."

"I can relate to what it feels like to be stranded at home with young children, all chafing at the bit to go out in the snow. But, in my case," Celeste said as she laughed, "I probably would have locked myself in the bathroom."

"Thank goodness Roberts turned to writing. Next, unbelievable as it may seem now, she went through the process of receiving one rejection letter after another. Can't you just picture this woman, writing her heart out, only to be told her work wasn't good enough? Try as she would, she couldn't generate enough interest in any of her properties. It was almost like the door had been closed to any more romance writers at that time. However, with determination, she plowed on and wrote and wrote and wrote. Think of the frustration that she must have felt. If it had been me, I don't think that I would have had the determination that Roberts had. Well, fortunately, then she wrote *Playing the Odds* and it became a best seller. Finally, she convinced her agent to let her write romantic, suspense novels under the pen name J. D. Robb. *Concealed in Death* is the latest one in this series. Since 1999 every one of her novels has been a *New York Times* Best Seller. Roberts is one amazing woman."

"Great report, Marty. Thanks so much. Wouldn't it be nice if we could get her to come here?" Celeste questioned.

"Do you want me to try?" Abigail asked.

Marty just about fell off her chair when she heard this. "What?"

"I know someone who knows her. If she can't come in person, maybe we could get her to participate on Skype."

"What a great idea, Abigail. We would appreciate your looking into this," an amazed Marty said.

"Not to change the subject, but I want to ask a question," Rosebud said. "What about the books we don't like? Would knowing anything about the author change our minds about the books? I don't think so. Anyway, now that I have thoroughly confused myself, I want to say that I enjoy knowing a bit about the authors, so I think we should continue our research," Rosebud stated.

"I totally agree with Rosebud," Celeste stated.

"Let's continue then with providing background information about the featured authors. Now, it's time to give your reports on the books you have read. Let's start with Celeste. Remember our process—we don't want a blow-by-blow description of what happened in the book you read. Just give a general overview," Marty directed.

When it was Abigail's turn to report on a book, she said, "I simply did not have time to read a book for this meeting. I had too many social obligations to meet," she sniffed.

Marty gave her a nice smile and moved on to the next member. When the others were finished, she thanked them for their participation. "Now, Jesse, will you please pull an author's card out of the box to determine our featured author for next month? Don't forget; it will also be your turn to do the research."

Jesse removed a card and said, "Oh, goodie! My favorite—John Grisham. I'm going to get his latest book, *Sycamore Road*. It was just featured in the *New York Times*."

"Okay, folks, see you next month. Abigail, could you please stay for a few minutes. I need to talk with you about another matter. It won't take long."

Abigail looked annoyed. After the room emptied out, she said, "Are you going to lecture me about not reading a book this time?"

"Oh, heavens, no. I realize what a busy woman you are. I love your idea about Roberts and if I can help in any way, please let me know. I want to discuss another one of your marvelous projects that I'm so excited about," Marty said eagerly.

Abigail finally smiled. "Oh, and what would that be?" she asked tactfully.

"I know that you are a firm believer in the power of music. So much, in fact, that you financially support a program at Smoker Elementary School for children who want to play in the band but can't afford to purchase an instrument. Abigail, this is amazing. Do you think that we could arrange for the children to come here—oh, say sometime in September or October—to play for us? Please say *yes*. I know that you don't want any publicity about all the nice things you do, but I think the children would enjoy making a presentation; and, with a roomful of grandmas and grandpas, what better audience could they possibly have? Please say *yes*, Abigail," Marty pleaded.

For once Abigail was speechless. "I never would have thought of that. I tell you what. I'll run this by William. He seems to have had so many interesting experiences, that I am certain he will know exactly how to put something like this together. If he thinks it's a good idea—then yes, I will certainly speak to the principal and Hortense about what we need to do to bring the children here. Oh, wouldn't it be a good idea to also have them here for lunch?"

As Abigail left the room, Marty was in shock. She had no idea that Abigail had already met with William. Even though Ellie May lived in the apartment next to William, she had never mentioned that she had heard any practice sessions between the singer and the piano player. *Operation Smile* simply could not have produced any change in Abigail's behavior this quickly. But, Abigail was definitely different today. When she mentioned William's name, her face softened and she smiled—something that, at least up to now, was rare for her. With no one else in the room, Marty mumbled, "God bless William." If their plan produced results so quickly, maybe they should go into the business of turning grouchy, arrogant people into lovable, pussy cats.

Looking at her watch, she realized that it was almost time for her granddaughter Laura to arrive with little Gretchen in hand. Marty was always happy to baby-sit Gretchen since it gave her an excuse to play with her dolls. And, surprisingly, it never bothered Marty when Gretchen would rearrange them, moving the dolls from one shelf to another. She just loved sitting on the bed with the child and making up stories about the dolls. Gretchen will be surprised when she sees that the bride doll is almost covered in diamonds.

She gathered her paperwork together. Glancing around the room to make certain that she hadn't forgotten anything, she reached for her cell phone.

"Ellie, Ellie, wait till you hear this...I just learned that *Operation Smile* is well on its way to be considered a full-blown success."

Chapter 7

William had arranged his sheet music in the order that Abigail had requested the other day. He had been surprised when he heard her sing the first time—she was fantastic. He had been apprehensive about playing for her ever since Nigel had told him about his one and only contact with Abigail. Somehow Nigel had offended her in some manner and she had demanded an apology—which he immediately had given her. It was obvious that Nigel didn't like the woman, but then, Nigel just did not appreciate most women. William was feeling very self-satisfied. There was the visit from Rosebud when it became clear that she liked him, and, now, there's Abigail. She had been very charming—not at all like Nigel had predicted. But this was their fourth and final rehearsal before their performance at the ladies' tea and he wanted everything to go right. He no longer thought of her as a stranger. Now, she was definitely a friend.

Wearing his new western shirt that he had ordered online, he adjusted his bolo tie while looking in the mirror. He turned his head back and forth, examining his face carefully. He could not be considered handsome, but William felt that he was probably better looking than most of the other male residents—but then, that wasn't saying much since many of them were much older than he was. He looked around the room, making certain that there was no clutter in sight.

When his doorbell rang, William smiled. He wasn't too sure why he felt this way. After all, he didn't really know Abigail very well and she might not like him at all.

"Ah, Abigail," he said as he opened the door. "You're right on time."

"Good morning, William. My, don't you like nice. It's always such a pleasure coming into your beautiful home. Your sense of style is amazing. It's reflected in the manner in which you dress and certainly in your decorating sense. Your living room has a warm, welcoming look."

"Coming from you—a woman of such good taste—that's a great compliment," William said.

Abigail's face lit up. "You know, William, if the rest of the men in this place only had half your manners, we ladies would be extremely fortunate," Abigail said as she handed William a saran-wrapped plate. "You mentioned the other day that you like whoppie pies, so I made some for you. One has vanilla filling, while the other is peanut butter."

"Thank you, Abigail. What a nice gesture. How can I repay you?" William said as he put the plate on the table.

"It is I who owe you a debt of gratitude for agreeing to play for me at the ladies' tea. Did you manage to find the sheet music you needed?" Abigail asked.

"You bet. I love the songs you have chosen. First, *Smoke Gets in Your Eyes* is a song that people love because it reminds them that they too have known deep, abiding love. Then, your second song, *Who's Sorry Now?* might bring back memories that sometimes lovers play games with one another. But, your last choice will be a surprise for our residents. Most of them will remember, *Are You Lonesome Tonight?*— *some* maybe on two levels—once when it first came out in the early 20s, and secondly, when Elvis Presley brought it back to life. The audience will absolutely love your program."

"No, William. Not my program—our program," Abigail said thoughtfully as she took her place alongside the piano.

William adjusted the sheet music. Abigail stood beside the piano. William had a difficult time focusing on his playing when Abigail began singing. He knew instantly that there would not be a dry eye in the house when she sang at the tea. He heard the words: *They asked me how I knew.....When a lovely flame dies, smoke gets in your eyes.* He had to turn his head so that Abigail wouldn't see that his eyes had welled up. Magic was happening—an undeniable excitement whenever she looked at him.

"Abigail, that was amazing," William said quietly.

Abigail positioned herself so that she was facing William. "I hope that the audience will feel the same way, William. Now, let's run over the other two songs one more time."

"Anything you say, Abigail, anything you say."

Abigail beamed.

Chapter 8

It was Friday afternoon and many of the residents were hurrying across The Square to Lilac Lane on their way to the welcoming party for their neighbors, Marie and Gordon Turnbull. Harry and Harvey Hamilton were hosting a party in their extra-large apartment. A bar was set up at one end of the living room where guests had their choice of drinks being served by a handsome, young bartender. Two young women were circulating with trays filled with all types of appetizers that the guests were enjoying. While Harry was making sure that everyone personally met the Turnbulls, Harvey was checking that the trays were being refilled and that no guest was without a drink.

Gordon, a tall, well-built Bahamian with silver hair, had a smile that was genuine. A former lawyer, Gordon looked the part even in the midst of a so-called casual party. His suit fit to perfection and his smile was genuine. He carefully guided his wife, Marie, by her arm so that she was constantly by his side. His soft British accent made him even more charming. Marie, was dressed a bit more casually. She wore a soft peach, silk tunic and black crepe slacks. Gold bangles were lined up on her right arm and large gold hoops dangled from her ear lobes. They were definitely a striking couple.

While the Turnbulls could afford to live almost anywhere, Marie loved Morning Glory Hill as soon as she had stepped in the front door. She had been impressed with the aura of friendship and family she sensed almost immediately. Several of Gordon's business associates had chosen to live at the very pricey retirement center just outside the city limits. But, according to Marie, that place was all fluff and no essence. Gordon wasn't quite sure that he agreed with his wife, but when it came to where they lived, she definitely had the final say.

"I would like to introduce you to Marty Miller. Marty, I am pleased to introduce you to Gordon and Marie Turnbull. Gordon recently retired from his law practice and Marie will be retiring from her clothing business at the end of the year." Harry said as he gestured toward the honored couple.

Marty shook Gordon's hand and then turned toward Marie. "Wait a minute," she said as her eyes opened wide. "Are you the Marie from *Marie's Closet?*

Marie was delighted. "How did you know?" she asked as she shook Marty's hand warmly.

"I just read an article about you in *Fashion Monthly*. While it mentioned that you were stepping down, I...well, I just don't know what to say. I have long admired your designs. You provide fashion that many can really afford. I can't believe that you're here. How lucky can we get, Harry? You must excuse me from rambling on, but I am so pleased to meet you...oh, I guess I already said that," Marty said, as she laughed nervously. "Oh, Mr. Turnbull, I'm pleased to meet you also; forgive my manners."

Gordon chuckled. "Nothing to forgive, Marty. And, please, call us Marie and Gordon. After all, we're neighbors. I agree with you, Marty—Marie is a talented woman. And, she showed her good taste by marrying me!" Gordon said as he gently touched his wife's arm.

"Ooh, go on Gordon. Marty, forgive my husband. He loves to tease. I guess that's rare these days—to find a lawyer with a sense of humor."

"Thank you very much, indeed. Solicitor, no more—just a retired husband," Gordon said mildly.

"I guess you are always hounded by people who are seeking free legal advice, but I have a friend that I would like to try to help. May I run something by you?" Marty asked Gordon.

"Of course, Marty. Just remember—whatever I say should be consider conjecture only. If your friend really needs legal advice, I can provide you with a contact person. Now, tell me the problem," Gordon reassured Marty.

"Well, my friend's husband has been dead for over a year now. She recently found some valuables that she didn't know he owned. Must she report this to the court?" Marty asked.

"It depends. Marty, your friend should seek legal advice so she can properly choose the right course of action. No matter what I say here, especially since I don't know the full extent of her findings, it could possibly be incorrect. It would be safer and more prudent for her to meet with a solicitor in private. Then, she'll be able to decide if she should report anything, or just keep it between herself and her solicitor," Gordon said as he winked his eye.

Chapter 9

William was looking forward to the big poker game tonight that was going to be held in his apartment. Nigel and he had approached several other male residents and an all-male poker club had been formed. While they agreed that some of the ladies might be interested in the game, they all felt that the women would inhibit and encroach on their fun. They wanted to be themselves, swear if they wanted to, and tell off-colored jokes. "Just the boys," as Nigel put it.

He rolled out his folding poker table from the closet and set it up in the middle of the living room. Earlier, he had gone to the store and stocked up on beer, beef jerky, and pretzels. Digging in the bottom drawer of his desk, he pulled out several decks of cards that he had purchased in Las Vegas last year. Like a bolt of lightning, it entered his head that perhaps he could invite Abigail to go with him to Vegas. As he crunched his eyebrows together, he thought that maybe he should wait until he was absolutely sure that she was interested in him. But, knowing women as he did, he had already spotted the signs that it might be possible to begin a relationship with her. What about Rosebud? After her visit the other week, he had assumed that she was interested in him. Smiling, he felt that he still had it—the magnetic pull. What did his grandson say the other day? Oh, yeah, he might be a chick magnet!

Nigel was the first to arrive, carrying a six-pack of Budweiser. "I wonder what Hortense, our fearless director, would say if she knew about this game? But, then again, I really don't care what that bossy woman thinks."

"Well, I sure as hell am not going to tell her," William said as he took the beer and put it in the refrigerator.

Harry, Samuel, Frank, and Gordon arrived and hurriedly took seats at the poker table.

"Doesn't Harvey play poker?" Samuel asked Harry.

"No, he doesn't like to play any kind of cards. He's sprawled on the sofa, reading a book," Harry replied.

"I'm not too sure Marie's happy that I'm here. This may cost me another piece of jewelry," Gordon said laughingly.

"Gordon, where did you meet your wife? Celeste mentioned that Marie used to live in Philadelphia," Nigel said as he leaned his elbows on the poker table.

"I was very lucky to meet her. The situation was brilliant. She came to the Bahamas on a business trip. All I needed was one smashing event to catch her eye, so I feigned interest in her business. And, as we say, the rest was history," Gordon said as he started shuffling the cards.

"William has had four wives," Nigel said, teasing his friend. "He woos them with his music. I guess I should have learned to play the piano," Nigel said a little sadly.

"I remember thinking I could play a piano, Frank said. "My uncle had a player piano and I use to put those paper rolls that had little holes punched in that created the music. I would pump away on the pedals like crazy and pretend that it was me striking those keys."

"My experience with music was really silly," Samuel said. I used to stand in front of the mirror and sing into my hairbrush and pretend that I was Vaughn Monroe singing *Racing With the Moon*. I guess I was doomed to be a boring, old history professor."

"Before we start," William said, "we need to come to an agreement on how we want this game to go. How about Dealer's Choice?"

They finally agreed with William. "I also recommend no more than three raises per hand. Is that okay with you guys?"

William saw to it that they each had a bottle of beer and he placed small tables with pretzels and beef jerky nearby.

Nigel shuffled the cards and announced, "Baseball, guys—threes and nines are wild and fours get an extra card."

The men were all enjoying themselves and the games seemed to get stranger and stranger. When it was Gordon's turn to deal, he said, "Sevens up, chums. Anyone getting a seven up is automatically out of the game. Sevens in the hole are wild."

"That's a kooky game," Nigel said. "It sounds like something the British would make up."

"Hello? Actually I learned this game from some of my American friends last month. I think it's brilliant," Gordon said as he smiled at Nigel.

"Think the ladies will get upset with us for not inviting any of them?" Frank asked.

"Well, they can start their own game if they really want to play," Nigel said. "Oh, I have a joke. There is this blonde who boards a plane and sits down in first class. The flight attendant asks to see her ticket and she shows it to her. So, the flight attendant says, 'You belong in coach, please take a seat there.' But the blonde replies, 'I am beautiful and I am going to New York City to become a famous model.' She stays put and just refuses to move. So, the flight attendant goes to the captain and tells him. He leaves the cockpit and whispers in the blonde's ear. The blonde gasps, immediately jumps up and runs back into the coach area and takes her seat. So, anyway, the flight attendant goes back in and asks the pilot what he said that made her move. 'Well, I told her that first class doesn't stop in New York City.' Nigel doubled up with laughter.

"Where do you get these silly jokes?" William asked.

"That's a secret," Nigel said, still wiping tears from his eyes.

As the evening wore on, the games got wilder and wilder and the empty beer bottles were stacking up. Every once in a while someone would tell a joke or make a quip, but surprisingly, most of them were not off-color. Paper money was stacked all around the table—ones, fives, tens and twenties. William kept an empty cigar box on the floor filled with cash just in case someone needed change.

"Let's call *The Night Owl* and order hoagies," Nigel suggested.

"Nigel, you've been stuffing yourself all night and you're **still** hungry?" William asked in disbelief.

"Sure. Playing cards always makes me hungry."

"How about we play one more round and then wrap it up for the night," Frank suggested.

"Okay." William said. "When the deal comes to me, I'll deal Showdown—seven cards, all up. Ten bucks each."

After his last guest left, William began straightening up his apartment. As he stacked all the beer bottles in the kitchen, almost without realizing it, his thoughts shifted to Abigail again. He wondered if she had felt the same kind of vibes that he had when she had stood beside him the other day at the piano. He tried telling himself that he was way too old to feel this way about anyone. Even with all his experience with women, whenever a new relationship had started, he always worried that the lady might not feel the same about him as he did about her. It would be nice, though, just to feel a soft hand take hold of his hand once again. He then remembered Rosebud. If he pursued Abigail, he just might be breaking Rosebud's heart. There were definitely some drawbacks to being a chick-magnet.

Chapter 10

William didn't want to be the first one to arrive at the Balance Class, so he lingered in The Square, reading the newspaper. He jumped as he felt someone take a seat beside him on the overstuffed sofa. "My God, Nigel, you scared me," he said as he turned to look at his friend. "Is something wrong? You look sad."

"Yes, an old friend of mine called me this morning to tell me he lost his job as night watchman at a local warehouse."

"Too bad. What happened?" William responded with genuine concern.

"Oh, he was replaced with something called a lock!" Nigel replied as he burst out laughing.

"Nigel, you're something else," William said with just a bit of annoyance in his voice.

"I sure am. Come on, William, you've got to admit that was funny," Nigel insisted.

William stood up. "Well, old boy, I hate to leave you, but I'm on my way to the Balance Class."

"Why? What's wrong with you, or do you just go there because so many women take that class?" Nigel teased.

William just shook his head and walked down the hallway to the gym. The instructor, Donald Cassel, had the chairs arranged in neat rows and was placing plastic stretch strips on each one.

"Good morning, William. Nice to see you again. What did you think of the class last week?" Donald asked.

"I enjoyed it very much," William replied. "Lately, I've been experiencing a bit of weakness in my legs that has made me a little unsteady at times. I decided to take your class as well as the exercise class that's held each Friday."

For the next fifty minutes, Donald kept the class moving. Standing, as well as sitting exercises, aimed at strengthening arms and legs, gave the class little time to concentrate on anything else. By the time the class was over, William was certainly ready to sit down. When Rosebud turned around in her chair and smiled at him, he was surprised that he felt guilty.

"I understand that your practice sessions with Abigail have been going very well. We're all looking forward to hearing the two of you perform tomorrow at the ladies' tea," Rosebud said as she smiled pleasantly.

"Thank you, Rosebud," was all that William could get out as he picked up his exercise equipment, tossed them into the bin, and hurried out the door. He quickly crossed The Square and headed for Daffodil Lane. His heart fluttered a bit when he spied Abigail, with clothing draped over her arms, at his front door.

"Oh, there you are, William. I was wondering if you could help me decide which dress to wear tomorrow. I want to compliment whatever you plan to wear," Abigail said, as she gently touched his arm.

William unlocked his front door and held it open as Abigail entered with a flourish. "I kind of like this one," she said as she held up a white cotton sheath that looked as light as a feather. Little pink flowers were scattered all over the dress and there was a touch of lace around the neckline.

"Abigail, that is eye-catching," William said softly. "I don't know much about ladies' attire, but I plan on wearing a white linen jacket and light beige trousers. If you wear that dress, I'll put a pink silk handkerchief in my pocket."

"All right, then. I'll see you tomorrow in the dining room around one. Will that be alright with you?"

"Abigail, why don't we walk over to the dining room now and let the manager know where we want the piano. You may also want to test the microphone to make sure that it does justice to your voice," William suggested.

"William, you think of everything. Perhaps you would allow me to buy you lunch at the *The Sassy Cat*. You have been so thoughtful," Abigail said considerately.

"Just put your dresses on the sofa and we can pick them up later. Come, my little song bird."

As they headed out the door, William reached for Abigail's hand—she didn't pull it away. Together, they walked down Daffodil Lane and crossed The Square, hand-in-hand. All along the way, they did not go unnoticed. Within five minutes, news of a newly-formed couple had spread all over Morning Glory Hill.

Chapter 11

Marty, and the other workers on the Tiptoe Thru The Tulips Tea committee, were headed for the dining room. Frank and Nigel were behind them, pulling a flatbed loaded with all sorts of items.

"Marty," Nigel asked, "do you really need all this stuff for a tea?"

"This isn't just a *tea:* this is a special occasion that we hope will become an annual event," Marty responded.

"Where should we put the flatbed?" Frank asked.

"Over there," Marty directed as she pointed to the area in front of the stage. "Gentlemen, we need seats for seventy-two guests. Don't put too much space between each table since I want it to be an intimate affair. Keep in mind, though, that we need space for the servers to get through."

"Where on earth did you find all these pieces of chinaware? They are attractive," Rosebud said as she examined the dishes. "Must we separate the patterns?"

"No, just mix them up. After you cover the tables with one of the flowered tablecloths, you can arrange the cups and saucers. I had them all washed yesterday so they are nice and clean. The tiered cake stands must go back to the kitchen. The teapots are already back there." Marty said. "Oh, and the sugar bowls and creamers go back there, too."

Marty stood in the center of the room, directing her helpers. Frank watched in awe. He couldn't take his eyes off her. Her poise and demeanor indicated that she was practical and organized. He was certain that there was nothing this amazing woman couldn't accomplish.

"What should we do next, Marty?" Frank asked.

"The florist delivered the tulips early this morning and they are near the loading dock. If you and Nigel could carry them in, that would be a big help," she said as she smiled at him.

Within a short time, the centerpieces of tulips were placed on the tables. In addition, large pots of tulips lined the front of the stage.

"Do you mean to tell me that all you women will be doing is drinking tea?" Nigel asked.

"Heavens, no," Rosebud said. "We will have scones, little cakes, and small cucumber sandwiches."

"Tell me that's a joke," Nigel said in disbelief. "Gees, I'm glad I wasn't invited!"

Just then, Barry Adams came out of the kitchen. "Hi, guys. The ladies have you working?" he teased.

"Like slaves," Nigel responded.

"Well, if you want to help some more, you can come to the kitchen this afternoon. We'll need some extra help when we begin to serve."

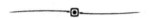

The guests for the tea began arriving around one-thirty. None of them were surprised to see that Sally was the first one in line. They had been asked to wear hats to this auspicious occasion, so Marty had spent a great deal of time shopping for hats for the three of them. Ellie May, who really didn't want to wear one, had finally selected a small, straw pillbox covered with tiny artificial violets. Rosebud, however, chose a large, floppy, woven straw with ribbons trailing down the back that she would swing back and forth every chance she got. Marty's choice was a sleek cloche that had tiny, sparkling gems, creating an aura of radiance around her face. Her hat added to the youthful look of her navy blue and white georgette dress.

Meanwhile, Celeste, volunteer librarian and scrapbook keeper, was following Harry around the room as he was snapping pictures. "Now, Harry, make certain that you get a picture of every table. I'm sure that many of the ladies will be requesting copies for their families," Celeste directed, "and I'll need plenty for our scrapbook. This is going to be a delightful occasion—one that we'll want to remember for a long time. So, try to capture everything."

"Yes, Celeste. I'm assuming that you'll want several pictures of Abigail and William?"

"Definitely. Oh, and our guest speaker, Marilyn Shoemaker from the *Daily Record*, will be here. Make certain that you get one of her alone and one with Abigail. Miss Shoemaker may be bringing her own photographer, but I want to be positive we have all the important shots."

Soon the room was filled with affable women wearing brightly-colored dresses. Even Ellie May had removed her traditional apron and looked years younger in her flowered garden dress. She was receiving many compliments from her friends—something she was not used to—but she loved every minute.

Mary Beth had left her reception desk and was standing beside the poster that indicated *Marie's Closet* was sponsoring today's tea. She greeted each guest by name as they entered the door. One-by-one she shook their hands and welcomed them warmly. Soft music was floating over the inter-com and Mary Beth would occasionally bob up and down in rhythm to the music. "Welcome, Betty Jane, oh, this must be your sister! You girls look like twins!"

"My goodness, Mary Beth—girls? It's been a long time since I was called that," Betty Jane said as she gave her sister a hug.

Mary Beth had something nice to say to everyone that only added to the over-all ambiance. "Isn't it nice how they closed off the rest of the room? It makes our spot here so warm and friendly. Don't you think?"

Soon the servers were moving about, placing beautiful tea pots on each of the twenty tables, along with 3-tiered trays of cookies, baklava, and assorted delights.

Just then, Marty approached the microphone. "It gives me great pleasure to welcome all of you to the first annual Tiptoe Thru the Tulips Tea."

Marty hadn't noticed that Frank had worked his way to a spot behind the curtains. He had been helping in the kitchen, along with Barry, filling tea pots and arranging the trays of food. When he saw Marty, he couldn't believe his eyes. He had never seen her look so pretty. He briefly thought he might be going out of his mind—a man his age, gawking at a woman. He never had been a ladies' man his entire life. He had lived and breathed his dairy farm—that is, until he sold it. None of his four daughters were interested at all in farming and his wife had died a long time ago. Now, the only things he had left of his beautiful farm were his memories and a lot of invested money. He jumped to attention when he realized that Marty was speaking.

"Our tea today is being sponsored by Marie Turnbull, owner of *Marie's Closet,* and fortunately a resident here at Morning Glory Hill. Let's give her a round of applause for her generosity." Marty paused while the crowed recognized Marie. "It gives me great pleasure to introduce Marilyn Shoemaker, editor of the Women's Section for the *Daily Record.* Marilyn has held this position for over ten years and we have all come to love her features and her columns. She is active in the community in all types of charity work and supports many organizations that focus on the needs of women and children. Please help me give a warm welcome to Marilyn Shoemaker."

With that, Frank left his hiding place and went back to the kitchen. Barry was busy wiping off tables. "Hey, Frank, what's going on out there?"

"A reporter from the newspaper is giving a speech. That's not my forte. I'd rather be helping you," Frank said rather sheepishly. "I do want to hear Abigail and William. You know, he's one hell of a piano player. Is it me or does Abigail seem different lately?"

"Abigail has always been a fine lady. But, yes, I must say she seems friendlier lately. Why, she has even offered her help with escorting perspective residents around our facility."

"Listen, that's Abigail singing. I must go," Frank said as he rushed off to his hiding spot. He hung onto the side of the curtain as Abigail began her first song. The chattering stopped. All eyes were fixed on Abigail as she began. Each word seemed to hit Frank right in his heart. He was not a man who cried—never—but he was certainly on the verge. When Abigail warbled her last '*smoke get in your eyes*' and bowed her head ever so gently, the audience rose to their feet and applauded.

"Thank you so much," Abigail said. "I must confess that I am an Elvis Presley fan. While some of his songs are not appropriate for my voice, a few of them are. William and I now present *Who's Sorry Now.* Of course, some of you may also remember this from either Patsy Cline's rendition or Connie Frances' recording."

For their last presentation, the two presented *Are You Lonesome Tonight?* When Abigail was finished, Willian stood up, walked over to Abigail, took her hand in his, and together, they bowed. Abigail's smile said it all—happiness—complete, utter happiness.

Just then, Frank lost his hold of the curtain and tumbled across the stage and landed directly at Abigail's feet. "Well, ladies, I must confess," Abigail said. "This is the first time that I have ever knocked anyone over with my singing!"

Without realizing it, William put his arm around Abigail and hugged her. The crowd went wild with applause.

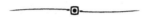

Later, when Marty was back in her apartment, she immediately kicked off her shoes and lay across her bed. She was pleased with how well everything had gone. Before she knew it, she had dozed off. In about twenty minutes, she woke up with a jolt. As she tried to get rid of her grogginess, her eyes began slowly to focus. As usual, she was looking for her favorite doll. She knew immediately that something was wrong. The necklace—it wasn't there! To be certain, she glanced around the shelf, but it was nowhere in sight. She looked through the folds of the doll's dress. She ran her hands back and forth on the shelf where the doll had been. Getting down on her knees, she looked under the bed. She even shook the bedspread, hoping that it had been caught between the spread and the blanket. Her heart began to sink. Where could the necklace be?

My God, I have been robbed! She didn't know what to do next. Her first instinct was to call 911, but that was out of the question. She had no paperwork to prove that she had ever owned a valuable piece of jewelry. Now her hands were shaking. Where could it be? Who could have taken it? What should she do?

She began pacing. Then, she remembered her expensive Googly-eyed doll. She breathed easier when she realized that the doll was in her usual spot. She looked over the rest of her collection and everything seemed to be in order. So, apparently, the only thing that had been taken was the necklace. Now what? Maybe I should tell Hortense. Bur I can't even prove I ever had the necklace.

Frank. Maybe he could help. But she would feel awkward going to him with this problem. I probably am to blame for this. I was suspecting Charlie of something—God only knows what. Now, I'm being punished for even thinking bad things about him.

As she closed her eyes, she pictured the necklace—three strands of diamonds interspersed with garnets, sparkling brilliantly, in a white gold setting. I might not ever see it again. Tears began to fall.

Tomorrow, she would call Ellie May and Rosebud. Together, maybe they would be able to figure things out—they always seem to anyway.

Chapter 12

Ellie May and Rosebud arrived together and simply walked into Marty's apartment.

"What on earth has happened, Marty? You sounded terrible on the phone," Ellie May stated.

"It's gone."

Rosebud and Ellie May said in unison, "What's gone?"

"I've got to tell you from the beginning. Sit down. This will take a while," Marty said on the verge of tears.

"Don't cry, Marty. We're here," Rosebud said encouragingly, as she patted Marty on her arm.

"Some time ago, I was cleaning out my husband's wardrobe and I found his old Dopp kit—I'm not sure it's called that but that's how he referred to it—you know where he kept his shaving stuff, toothbrush, and things like that. Well, anyway, I was just about to toss it in the trash when I felt something in the bottom, under the lining. I almost fell over when I discovered a diamond necklace."

"What?" Rosebud said. "My God, Marty, what did it look like?"

"I'll try to draw it on my legal pad," Marty replied. "It had three strands, like this," she said as she began sketching. "And, in the middle of each strand, there were several other gems—I think they were garnets. But I really don't know anything about precious stones," Marty said with a little sob in her voice.

"Did it look as if it was worth a lot of money?" Rosebud quizzed.

"I think it was—but I'm not sure. It could have been fake. I'm just not certain," Marty reiterated.

"Diamonds are judged on cut, color, clarity, and carat weight. Here, look at my ring. Do you think each diamond in the necklace was about this large?" Rosebud asked.

"Gee, I can't say. Maybe they were a bit smaller. Oh, my, I'm no help at all," Marty said as she hung her head down.

"Now, Marty, don't get upset. Let's assume that the diamonds were real," Rosebud suggested.

"Can you think of any reason that Charlie would have put a valuable necklace in his Dopp kit?" Ellie May asked.

"My Charlie knew some shady people and I had often wondered if they were into anything illegal. Maybe it was something he won in a card game, but then again, they wouldn't have used anything that pricey in a poker game, would they?" Marty asked hopefully.

"I doubt that, Marty," Rosebud said. "Maybe he got it for you and simply forgot all about it."

"I don't think so," Marty said. "I wanted to show it to you *so* many times, Rosebud, since you know your jewels, but I was afraid."

"Afraid of what?" a puzzled Rosebud asked.

"I couldn't think of a reason why Charlie would have diamonds. I don't know, Rosebud, I was so confused when I saw it that I just didn't know what to think. When I went to the party to welcome the Turnbulls, I approached Gordon, seeking his legal advice."

"What did he say?" Rosebud asked.

"I told him that a friend of mine found valuables that she hadn't declared when she had settled her husband's estate. He recommended that the lady hire an attorney, who could then look over the valuables and advise her on the right procedure," Marty said as she laid her legal pad on the table.

"Well, you can't do that now—you don't have the necklace. Do you have any idea how long the necklace has been missing," Rosebud asked.

"Absolutely no," Marty said forlornly.

"I have an idea. Hand me that legal pad, Marty. Let's list the reasons that Charlie might have had for hiding the necklace in his kit," Rosebud said. "If we see the reasons in print, perhaps it will give us a better picture of why it was placed there."

Ellie May made the first suggestion. "Maybe one of his friends stole it and asked Charlie to hide it. Now, Marty, remember, these are only ideas."

"I hate to say this," Rosebud said, "but maybe it could have been a gift for another woman."

"Maybe it was supposed to be a gift for me," Marty quickly added.

"Oh," Ellie May said, "maybe he planned to use it for a nest egg— you know."

"If he was connected to the mob, maybe they were going to use it for a pay-off," Rosebud added.

"Alright, now let's come up with ideas of what could have happened to it," Ellie May offered.

"Did you have anyone come into your apartment to do any work for you—like housecleaning or maintenance work?" Rosebud asked.

"A couple of weeks ago, I used a cleaning lady that my granddaughter recommended. Oh, last week I had one of our maintenance people here hang some pictures and repair a door for me. But they were both nice people. I doubt that either one of them could have taken it," Marty argued.

"Okay. Let's start with the cleaning lady. Let's look into her background and see if we can find anything suspicious," Rosebud suggested.

"I feel terrible—I really don't like spying on people," Marty added.

"You say you'can't go to Hortense or the cops because you have no proof that you ever owned a necklace, so we can't get them involved. The three of us can work together and maybe we can solve this without getting anyone else involved. After all, Marty, we're not going to allow them to cart you off to prison," Ellie May offered.

"My God, Ellie May. Who said she would go to prison? Maybe she would be in trouble as far as inheritance taxes were concerned, but it certainly wouldn't rise to the level of prison," Rosebud stated firmly.

"You don't know. I've seen some brutal things on TV involving cops and making arrests and such. I am not going to allow them to handcuff her and take her away," Ellie May said with a sob in her voice.

"Ellie May, how sweet. Let's start with a small investigation and see where it goes. I'll look some things up on the Internet and then we'll get started. You know, as long as we can keep you safe, Marty, this whole thing should be fun!" Rosebud said.

"I surely hope so—I really don't look good in stripes!" Marty said as she smiled for the first time. Thumbing through her phone book, she said, "Here it is. Her name is Susan Reed and she lives over on Clydesdale Road. Now, how do we begin?"

"Look," Rosebud said almost in a whisper. "Let me begin this by myself. I'll keep you both posted so you'll know what's happening. I have someone who can investigate people without them knowing it. My husband and I used him when we wanted to look into some of the jewelers that we dealt with. This guy is discrete. He knows how to ferret out deep, dark secrets held by people."

"What about the cost?" Marty inquired.

"This guy owes me a lot. If I need money, I'll let you know. Meanwhile, I'm going to put my wheels into motion," Rosebud announced as she bounced out the door.

Chapter 13

Frank pulled his bathrobe around him and tied the sash. As he headed out his apartment door, he chuckled at the very thought of his walking down Orchid Lane on his way to *The Night Owl* at midnight. He felt a bit like a naughty school boy, sneaking out on his parents to meet his friends down by the swimming hole to smoke cigarettes. Since he moved into Morning Glory Hill, he had never done anything quite this silly. Silly was not in his nature.

Having no idea if anyone else would be this foolish to be wandering around the halls so late at night, he decided to look at this as an adventure. With a spring in his step, he crossed The Square that was deserted and was pleased to see the little open sign above the doorway to the late night eatery. As he turned into the small shop, he was shocked to see Nigel and William seated at a small marble-topped table.

"Well, you're a stranger here," Nigel said, as he pulled out a chair for Frank. "Can't sleep, buddy?"

"Just a bit hungry," Frank said. "Do you guys come here often this late at night?"

"Nigel is here a lot," William said. "He's an owl. He even looks a bit like one," William said as he laughed.

"This may surprise you, but I really like the quiet. I can stretch out, get my hot chocolate and a doughnut, and just be me. No worry about displeasing the ladies. I can just be plain, old Nigel."

"Does someone actually work here? Do they get customers often?" Frank inquired.

"Yes, and yes," William said. "Andrew Cutler, an ex-jockey, works the night shift here. He does the baking for the restaurant. We all call him Stretch. Seems he got that name in grade school. I guess the kids teased him about being so short. He has to stand on a platform to reach some of the ovens in the kitchen. But, he's a hellava good baker."

"I'm glad to hear that," Frank said, "I love my goodies."

"Frank, may I ask you a question?" Nigel said. Then, without waiting for a reply, he said, "What did you do before you moved here?"

"I had a dairy farm. Keeping up with that as well as raising my four daughters kept me quite busy." Frank replied.

"Wow, four girls! I've been a bachelor my whole life. Seems that the women just don't know how to handle a handsome specimen like me," Nigel quipped.

"That sure is an overstatement, my friend," William said.

"What about you, Nigel. What's your background?" Frank asked.

"I worked for Sunset Properties. I was in charge of all their properties in the northeast part of the good old USA. I really liked my job and I thought long and hard before I retired. They were good to me—good pay—good retirement—good health coverage," Nigel said. "Of course, they were good to me because I performed my duties very well, too. I am a firm believer that when you work for someone, you give that person one hundred percent of yourself. I simply just didn't have enough time to get involved with women."

"And you, William?" Frank inquired.

"I was in the music business. Nothing spectacular. A few bands here and there," William replied.

"Don't forget," Nigel interrupted, "you also got married four times."

"We'd be here all night long if I talked about *that* part of my life," William said.

Just then they spied a figure walking towards them. "By God, I think that's Jessie. Watch out for her cane—she uses it to nudge people—I hate that," William said.

"Good evening, gentlemen," Jessie said as she bounced her cane on the floor.

"Hello, Jessie. What are you up to tonight?" Nigel asked.

"Well, I guess the same thing you gentlemen are up to," Jessie said with a mischievous smile.

As Nigel glanced at his watch, he said, "I got here yesterday."

"Oh, I doubt that," Jessie said.

"It's true—I got here about a half hour before midnight. That makes it yesterday now," Nigel argued.

"Look, today is today, not tomorrow," William stated firmly.

"But, if I came here yesterday, then it has to be tomorrow," Nigel said curtly.

"When you came in here, it was today's yesterday," William retorted.

"That's silly. What happened to tomorrow?" Nigel argued.

"It can't be yesterday now," Frank argued.

"Well, it can't be tomorrow since tomorrow never comes," William added.

"But if tomorrow never comes, then how do we ever get today?" Nigel said as he crossed his arms in front of his chest in righteous indignation.

"Tomorrow isn't here yet. There is an old saying, *tomorrow never comes,* and that makes sense," William insisted.

"Maybe to you, but not to me," Nigel argued.

The four of them were quiet for a few minutes. They appeared to be listening to the sounds emanating from the kitchen as Stretch moved his baking pans around.

"By the way," Nigel said, "did you hear that a burglar broke into *Marie's Closet,* the dress shop on Commonwealth, and took a dress? And, then he had the nerve to come back the next day."

"But why did he come back the next day?" Jessie asked as she shook her head.

"Wrong size," Nigel replied loudly as he doubled up in laughter.

William and Jesse were still rolling their eyes as Stretch came out of his kitchen. "You folks like some warm buns?" he asked. "I just made some doughnuts that are ready for icing and sprinkles—any takers?"

"Yes, Stretch, I would like a bun today, not tomorrow, nor yesterday, but today," Nigel said as he chuckled. "Jessie, I've got a question for you. What's with you rhyming all the time?"

"I used to run a child care center and I would rhyme to amuse the children. I felt that it taught them lots of new words, and they always seemed to have fun with the idea of rhyme. Does that annoy you, Nigel? I apologize if it does."

"Sometimes. But then I guess I annoy people sometimes, too."

"Sometimes!" William said loudly. "You annoy me all the time, friend."

"I know you don't mean that," Nigel said. "We're buddies. But maybe now that you're sweet on Abigail, you may forget all about me."

Jessie's eyebrows went up. "Have I missed something?" she asked coyly.

"Oh, it's the latest gossip. Was your head in the clouds that you didn't hear it?" Nigel asked.

"Guys. Wait just a cotton-picking minute. Abbie and I are friends. Okay?" William added.

"Okay," Nigel replied. "Remember, though, there are friends, and then there are *friends*. Get my meaning, Jessie?"

"Sure do, friend," she said, as they all laughed. *"While just friends for today, tomorrow, who's to say?"*

It was almost two in the morning when Frank got back to his apartment. He was glad that he had gone to *The Night Owl*. It was a rare time of fun for him—having a good time with other residents. His daughters would be surprised to know that he had been part of a group—maybe even what they call an *in-group*. As he walked by the sofa table, he glanced at the photos of his girls. They were not like him in any way. His girls were out-going—making friends everywhere they went. Maybe it was time he followed his daughters' lead. Time for work is over. As he closed his eyes, he thought about Nigel. *If tomorrow never comes, then how do we have today?*

Chapter 14

The necklace had been missing for three days now and Marty was getting anxious. Rosebud had cautioned Marty that her private investigator would be taking his time to do his job correctly, so she lectured herself that she had to be realistic in her expectations. Since she really liked Susan as a person, Marty didn't want her to be involved in taking the necklace. After all, the damned thing might just be a phony piece of jewelry, anyway...but, what if it was real?

Once again, probably for the hundredth time, she examined her doll case. Each time she did this, she wanted to find the necklace even more. But it had not magically appeared. She wished now that she had just tossed the Dopp kit away and that she had never found that damned thing. The whole experience had been too much for her. She wanted her old, boring existence back again.

While she was proud that the tea had been such a rousing success, she felt that the necklace had somehow robbed her of enjoying the afterglow. The local newspaper had done a superb job covering the party. Her phone was constantly ringing with women calling her for shepherding the entire affair and expressing a hope that this would become an annual event.

As she glanced at her calendar, she realized that she had another important activity to get underway. She needed to look into getting Nora Roberts to participate in some kind of activity for the book club. Technology was certainly not her bag, so she needed to talk to Barry Adams, who was not only the Activities Director for Morning Glory Hill, but he was also their resident expert when it came to technology. While she was not opposed to the use of technology, she much preferred hands-on and live sessions with authors rather than just talking to a screen. Perhaps she could contact some of the other book clubs in the area and they could jointly support some type of author conference. The new city conference center would be an ideal place to hold a bang-up seminar that might even draw readers from across the state. As long as she was going to do something, it may as well be super-big and dramatic. That would surely get her mind off that blankety-blank necklace.

As she approached The Square, she spotted Barry holding court with several residents who were looking at some travel brochures. "Look these over, and if any of you would like additional information, come see me or give me a call. I'm familiar with all the ships as well as the cruise lines. I can assure you that you'll have first-class accommodations, gourmet food, quality entertainment, and well-appointed casinos."

"Barry, could I have a few minutes of your time?" Marty asked.

After they were settled in Barry's office, he said, "Now, how can I help you?"

"I was thinking of having a symposium that would focus on books and reading. I'm not sure that we could handle that here, or whether we would need to use the conference center downtown."

"Marty, you must be a psychic! I just got word that such an event will be scheduled for late next year. Nothing is definite yet. Borders Books, along with three, small local book stores, will be the sponsor. I suggest that you contact Borders and offer your assistance. You are such an organized person—so adept at putting things like this in order—that I believe they would welcome you with open arms. Tell you what. I'll call my friend at Borders and give him your name—that is—if that's okay with you?"

"Certainly, Barry." Marty said as she got up to leave. As she opened the door, William almost fell in. "Oh, Marty, perfect timing. I want to speak to you and Barry if you both have a few minutes."

"Sit down, folks," Barry encouraged.

"Abigail and I have come up with an idea. We were talking with a group of our friends and the topic of high school proms came up. Only one of us had ever attended a prom. So, we thought: why can't we hold a prom here?" William asked as he waited for their reactions.

"Marvelous" Marty said. "What a nice idea. But, it will take a great deal of planning to pull something like that off. I'll have a zillion questions to ask you,"

"Zillion or not, I think the two of us, along with three or four others, could serve as the planning committee. What about you, Barry?" William asked as he leaned forward in his chair. "Would Morning Glory Hill be willing to fund such an event?"

"Sounds good. Morning Glory Hill can certainly be the sponsor, but I'll need a resident committee to help. If you have Marty as the chair of the committee, your prom will be a rousing success," Barry offered. "Of course, I'll serve as the representative for Morning Glory Hill, but it will really be up to the residents to pull it off. I can certainly arrange for a live orchestra of some sort. You may want to do something like choosing a King and Queen, and even awarding door prizes."

"William, we have to think about who we want to serve on the committee. We need people who will be willing to work hard," Marty said. "Let's go find a quiet spot and get started."

As they walked across The Square, Rosebud was just coming in the front door. "Marty, Marty," she called. "I need to speak to you for a minute in private," she said excitedly.

Pulling Marty's arm, Rosebud whispered, "She just bought a new car."

"Who bought a new car?"

"Susan—your cleaning lady."

Chapter 15

Ellie May filled three coffee cups and placed them on her kitchen table. "Here, we might need this. Now, tell me from the top, what you found out, Rosebud."

"All my friend discovered so far is that Susan just purchased a new car. And, she didn't need financing. What do you think that could mean?" Rosebud asked as she nodded her head.

"But," Marty said, "a car may not be connected to my missing necklace. Was it a brand new car?"

"Yes. A Prius, may I add," Rosebud said convincingly.

"Someone could have paid for her car. You know, like a boyfriend, or something," Marty replied.

"Oh, come on now. She's not *that* good-looking," Rosebud said.

"Rosebud, that was nasty," Marty said. "Susan isn't a beauty, but she's a nice person," Marty argued. "She not only works as a cleaning lady; she's also a server at the up-scale *Serenity.*"

"Wow, they say that's really a posh restaurant. Are you saying that she could have purchased a new car on her tips?" Rosebud asked.

"Well, no, but gee...I was hoping that she hadn't taken the necklace," Marty said.

"If I may interject here, what do you say we do some investigation on our own?" Ellie May suggested.

"Like what?" an agitated Rosebud said.

"Well, why don't we take a trip to *Serenity* and just nosey around?" Ellie offered. "You know, *case the joint.*"

"What do you think we'll find out there?" Rosebud asked.

"I'm not sure," Ellie May replied. "But, perhaps, we may discover the answer to how she could afford to pay cash for a new car. You'll never know what you can find out if you just ask the right questions. How about it?"

"I do know she said that she works there Friday and Saturday nights. How about going there on Friday for dinner? I'll drive," Marty said.

"I can't get over all this," Ellie May said. "We just found out that there's going to be a prom—imagine me at a prom. And, now, we are actually playing detectives. I wonder what will be next."

"Maybe we might get in over our heads. Let's review what we know so far," Marty encouraged. "I have no proof that I ever had an expensive necklace."

"Are you certain about that?" Rosebud asked.

"Only Gretchen and I actually saw it," Marty replied.

"Gretchen? Your great granddaughter?" Rosebud asked.

"When I found it, I put it on my bride doll—the one Charlie gave me so long ago. When I babysat Gretchen, I showed it to her."

"Well, she's too young to testify that you had a necklace. Did anyone else see it?" Rosebud inquired.

Marty shook her head. "You two only have my word for it," Marty said sadly.

"Marty, we believe you. I can assure you," Ellie May said convincingly.

"You know, it could have disappeared any time after that day," Marty said. "The only other person that was in my apartment was Preston, the maintenance man."

"Let's not even consider him until we rule out Susan," Rosebud suggested.

"Before I leave, Ellie May, I brought you some clothing catalogs so you can get an idea of the kind of gowns currently being offered," Marty said.

"I thought we planned to go to *Marie's Closet* tomorrow?"

"Yes, we are. I just thought it might give you an opportunity to browse without the two of us bugging you," Marty said as she placed the stack of catalogs on the table. "Meanwhile, I'll get a reservation for us for Friday night at *Serenity*."

After Rosebud and Marty left, Ellie May poured herself another cup of coffee. She really should cut back on her caffeine—this would be her fifth cup for the day. Sliding into her favorite overstuffed chair, she stretched her legs out and let out a sigh of relief. It felt good just to get off her feet for a while. She wasn't used to taking time to look at catalogs, especially those featuring women's clothes. It had been a long time since she needed something new. She hated to admit it, but she was excited about the prospect of going to a prom—even though she wouldn't have a date—a thought that disturbed her; but she wasn't sure why.

When she spotted something that she might want to review, she would dog-ear the page. So many of the dresses were either cut way too low, split up to you-know-what, or they were ruffled everywhere. She wasn't about to show any cleavage. Since Marty was taking her to *Marie's Closet*, a high-priced dress shop that she had never visited, she had already made up her mind that she was not going to worry about any price tags. This might be the last time that she would splurge on a silly dress. After all, she deserved to get something that she really liked. Suddenly she stopped paging. She could not understand what she was looking at. At first, she thought that they were pieces of art—strange looking pieces of different shapes and colors. Pulling her brows together, she pulled the catalog in front of her face so she could read the fine print. Words such as <u>pleasure</u>, <u>massager</u>, and <u>climaxer</u> were in bold print. Then it struck her. She was so shaken that the pile of catalogs slid off her lap onto the floor. She let out a gasp. She had heard about things like this, but she had never seen them. She practically flew out her front door and hurried over to Lilac Lane, waving the catalog in front of her. Bursting through Marty's front door and shoving the catalog at Marty, Ellie May was now in tears.

"Ellie May, what's the matter?" her friend asked.

Ellie couldn't speak. Instead, she handed the catalog to Marty, all the time shaking her head back and forth. When Marty realized what had upset her friend so much, she started laughing. "Oh, my, I forgot about this catalog. They always advertise sex toys all the way in the back of the magazine. I'm sorry it disturbed you so much, Ellie May."

"How can they put such things in print, let alone in a catalog advertising ladies' clothes. I wouldn't buy anything from those people," Ellie May sobbed.

"Now, now. Just sit down and catch your breath. Please don't be upset. I'm so sorry. I just ignore those pages, but I should have realized that you would find them upsetting."

"More than upsetting. I find them disgusting," Ellie May said as she was slowly regaining her composure. "I'm not angry with you, Marty, honestly, I'm not. I know that I'm old-fashioned. It just shocked me."

"Did you find anything in the other catalogs that you liked?"

"Not really." Ellie May then lowered her head and said, "Please don't tell anyone about this. I don't want everyone to know how dumb I am. I bet that repulsive Nigel knows all about stuff like that. And, heaven forbid, I surely don't want Abigail to know. She already looks down her nose at me. But Nigel bothers me more."

Marty leaned forward, took Ellie May's hand, and gently said, "Tell you what. When you are annoyed with Nigel, just think about how ridiculous he looked in those ant shorts!"

Chapter 16

Rosebud was taking her time getting dressed to go to dinner at *Serenity*. After all, it wasn't every day that she got out in the great wide world that lay beyond Morning Glory Hill. Since she had given up her driver's license last year, she had to wait for her son to take her places or hitch a ride with someone else. She finally decided on a white silk, ruched blouse to offset her black crepe, ankle-length skirt. Whenever she wore this particular outfit, she felt years younger. Grabbing her small, beaded clutch bag, she hurried out the door to meet Ellie May and Marty.

As she climbed into Marty's Malibu, she said, "Ladies, isn't this fun? We're dressed to the nines and out for the evening—just like when we were young."

"Rosebud, we never went out together when we were young. My goodness, my mother wouldn't have allowed me to go anywhere unless I was properly chaperoned," Ellie May said.

"We won't need chaperones tonight," Rosebud said. "I'm really excited about snooping on Susan."

"Oh, my, I didn't think of it that way. I'm not too sure that I should be doing this," Ellie May said hesitantly.

"Wasn't it you who said that you wouldn't allow the cops to take Marty to prison? How are we going to protect her unless we unravel the mystery of the diamond necklace?" Rosebud challenged.

"Now, let's just look at this as getting to know Susan better. You know, be casual and forget about the detective stuff," Marty suggested.

The front door of the restaurant opened automatically and a handsome young man greeted them warmly. "Welcome to *Serenity*, ladies. Do you have reservations?"

"Yes, we do. Miller is the name. Would it be possible for us to sit in Susan's section? She's a friend of ours," Marty asked.

"Certainly, right this way, ladies."

Ellie May was having a difficult time following the *maître d'* since she was trying to look at the décor. Absentmindedly, she took the menu he handed her. "This place is beautiful. Look, there's a stream that runs over a little waterfall. And the plants—look, they're everywhere. Rosebud, look over there. I have never seen such an elegant place— statues, art work, and the colors—so gorgeous."

"Well, from the looks of this place, Susan must earn good tips. I can't wait to see the prices on the menu," Rosebud remarked.

"Hello, Mrs. Miller. How nice to see you again. I was thrilled when I saw it was you," Susan said.

"Susan, I want you to meet Mrs. Dunkel and Mrs. McClaren. They also reside at Morning Glory Hill."

"Nice to meet you, both. Would you like to begin with a cocktail?" Susan asked.

"If it's alright with you two, I would like to order a bottle of Richardson's Cabernet," Marty said. "Will that be okay, or do you prefer something else?"

Hearing agreement from the others, Susan hurried away and the ladies began looking over the menu.

"I wonder who that man is over there," Rosebud said as she pointed to a distinguished- looking man who seemed to be wandering around the restaurant. "Maybe he's the owner. He seems to know a lot of people."

Rosebud was piqued at the thought that perhaps this man had some connection with Susan. After all, he was rather handsome and, if he owned the place, probably also wealthy—someone who could afford to buy someone else a car. She decided that he would be her target for tonight.

Soon, the diners were enjoying their wine as they tried to make a selection from the extensive menu. Rosebud was surprised at the prices—they weren't as high as she had thought they would be. In order to watch her target, she held her menu up just high enough so she could keep her eye on the man. She swallowed hard when she realized that he was heading their way.

"Good evening, ladies. Welcome to *Serenity*," he said with a slight southern twang. "Is this your first time here?"

"Yes, it is," Marty said, taking command of the table. "We're friends of Susan,"

"Ah, Susan," he said. "She is a charmer, isn't she?"

Rosebud's eyebrows went up a bit. "We think so," she replied. "And, you are?"

"Oh, sorry, I'm Fredrick Knoblauch. My wife and I are the owners. I hope you enjoy your evening. Please, let Susan know if you need anything."

As he walked away, Rosebud smiled. "He's guilty," she said with conviction.

"What? Guilty of what?" Marty asked.

"He's seeing Susan on the side. I can tell," Rosebud insisted.

"For goodness sake, Rosebud, you only just met the man and you don't know much about Susan either. How can you say that?" Marty asked.

"I know. I just know. I watched his eyes as he talked about her."

Rosebud wanted to concentrate on Fredrick and Susan, so she drifted away from their conversation. If she could see them together, then she would know for certain. She would be on the alert for *the look*—the one lovers exchange when they think no one else is watching. But, if those two are lovers, that could rule Susan out as being a thief—it would make her a mistress. It could also be possible that she is both—a thief and a mistress. Suddenly, she spotted Susan hurrying through a small door near the waterfall. In just a few seconds, Fredrick went out the same door. Ah, now Rosebud was certain.

While Rosebud was enjoying her dinner, she was still keeping her eyes on Fredrick and Susan. She had learned this trick long ago when she had felt that her husband might be cheating on her. That's why Rosebud had fired that two-bit hussy who had been trying to steal her man from right under her nose in their jewelry store. From then on, Rosebud had been very careful when she hired female clerks. Apparently, she was very good at selecting the right personnel, since Rosebud and her husband had celebrated fifty years of marriage shortly before his death.

Later, when Susan returned to the table, she was pushing a cart that was filled with luscious- looking desserts. "Oh, Susan, I know this isn't the proper time or place, but I have a question for you. Would you be able to clean my apartment the next time you come to Morning Glory Hill to take care of Marty's place?" Rosebud asked.

"Oh, I'm no longer providing cleaning services. I picked up more hours here at the restaurant. I was going to call you on Monday, Mrs. Miller, to tell you this and to thank you for your past business. I owe you an apology."

"I'll miss you, Susan," Marty said. "You surely don't owe me an apology."

"My schedule here will be quite full and, along with that, I'll be moving in just a few days," Susan replied. "My life seems to be changing so rapidly that I sometimes find it difficult to keep my head on straight. My mom used to tell me that the one thing that is constant is change. I now know what she meant."

"I wish you good luck," Marty said convincingly.

"I'm so excited about moving since I'll be living at Kensington Place."

When Susan said this, Rosebud's eyebrows went up. "I hear that it's very fashionable," she said. "I also understand that there's a waiting list to get in there. Rumor has it that you must know someone who knows someone."

Susan laughed. "Well, yes, I do. Ladies, how about dessert?"

Rosebud knew in her gut that she was right about Fredrick and Susan: It is not an assumption any more—a little love nest for the fornicators! Now we may not have to investigate that maintenance man who had been in Marty's apartment. It seems very clear who took that necklace. But, if we find that we must handle two investigations at one time, it may get complicated. We pulled off *Operation Smile*, so this should be a piece of cake!

Chapter 17

William was the first to arrive at Marty's apartment for the initial meeting of the Prom Committee. Abigail had given him several good ideas that he wanted to run by the others. He had suggested that she serve on the committee, too, but she wouldn't hear of it. He didn't know what he would do without her. He felt extremely lucky to have found her. And, as he told Nigel the other day, even luckier that Abigail obviously thought well of him. And, there was the kiss—a kiss on the cheek last night when she had left his apartment—something that he surely didn't share with Nigel.

All the residents whom William and Marty had asked to serve on the committee had readily agreed. Celeste Mayfair, the volunteer librarian; Frank Snyder, who had made himself known to William one late night at *The Night Owl;* Harvey Hamilton, a retired events coordinator whom they knew had lots of experience in putting together elegant events; Sally Fisher, who claimed that she had served as a chaperone for so many senior proms that she could recite chapter and verse on each one, and Barry Adams, who would serve as representative of Morning Glory Hill.

In no time at all, the others arrived. As they each took a seat, Marty served iced tea and homemade cookies. As usual, Sally, leaning across Celeste to be the first one to get to the plate of cookies, took a handful. Marty, chuckling at Sally's behavior, sat down and said, "Thank you for being so prompt. William and I have been talking about a prom committee and we think that we should begin our work by selecting a chairperson, a treasurer, and a publicist. How does that sound?"

"Far be it from me to tell you talented people how to run this committee, but I think William would make an excellent chairperson. I would also like to recommend Frank for treasurer, and Harvey for publicist. But, here I go again, putting my two cents worth in before anyone else has had an opportunity to volunteer. I apologize," Barry said.

"You realize that you put all men in charge of the prom, don't you? I think you need to have Marty serve as co-chair so that we women don't get overlooked," Celeste said rather firmly. "After all, the three of us have all been to proms, so we're not completely ignorant about the topic."

"But, Celeste, we are part of the committee and we are not shy. Believe me, our ideas and suggestions will be heard," Marty said as she laughed. "I'll serve as co-chair but, William, I will depend on you to run the meetings."

"Okay, then," William said. "Let's begin by deciding the major areas of concern. We can list them on this flip chart and that will help us take on our concerns one-by-one."

Soon, they were all offering ideas and they finally settled on a dozen different areas.

"I think the first thing we should do is pick a name and a theme for the dance. Celeste has suggested *Senior Prom* and I think that would be appropriate. After all, that's what they call a high school prom and we are, for sure, all seniors—just a different kind of seniors now."

"That's a good idea," Marty added. "I'm not sure about the theme, but perhaps we could use something like, wait...how about we use morning glories in some fashion? You know, they will be in bloom at that time; so our theme could be *A Night at Morning Glory Hill.* Of course, our theme needs to be morning glories. You know, this place was built on a hill that used to be covered with morning glories."

"Wow, I really like that idea," William said. "If we all are in agreement, we have our name and our theme." William paused for a minute. Hearing only good comments, he said, "Okay, now let's pick a date. Barry, we need your help. You probably know what activities are in the works and what dates we should avoid. Remember, we need a lot of time to put all this together."

"I assume we're having a formal prom?" Celeste asked. She glanced at the men, and then said, "That will mean a dark suit or a tux for the men, Oh, a white dinner jacket will also be appropriate."

"Barry, what about the last Saturday in June?" William asked.

After checking his electronic calendar, Barry said, "That will work. Nothing has been scheduled for that date here. I know that *The Melody Makers* have a standing commitment for every Friday at some club. But I'll check with them regarding the date you want."

"I never heard of that group," Marty said. "Do they play music that our residents will like?"

"I don't want that bang, bang stuff," Sally added.

"Bang, bang?" Frank asked.

"You know, when people are screaming or doing that thing called *rap* and you can't understand anything they are saying," Sally explained. "I may be fat, but I still want to dance."

"I have some questions to ask," Frank said.

"Shoot," William responded.

"I remember helping my daughters get ready for proms and it was quite an ordeal until they got their dresses and shoes together. But, I also know that they had beaus who picked them up, gave them corsages, and escorted them to the dance. Will our prom be the same?"

William chuckled. "I guess it *was* chaotic for you, Frank. I don't know how you survived with four daughters to look after. You probably had to sit by your front door with a shotgun to keep all the boys away."

"It was tough at times—especially after Emma died. But, my sister helped from time to time. I used to think that I would enjoy the quiet when they all left the nest, but I was so wrong. Did you ever know that silence can be deafening? I finally had enough of talking to the walls, so when I got a great offer for the farm and the other land I owned nearby, I took it. So, here I am."

"Wow, four girls. You deserve a medal," Barry said.

"At one time, I thought that maybe one of them would come back home to live. But, that never happened. I'd like to think that I could take credit for that—you know, for encouraging independence. But, I have another question about the prom. Must our residents come as couples?" Frank inquired.

Marty smiled. "No, Frank. We certainly have more women here than men, so most of the women will be coming in small groups. However, you gentlemen are certainly encouraged to invite a lady of your choice if you wish."

William was pleased that the group was working so well together. Within three hours, they had discussed all the areas and assigned responsibilities. "Harvey, when can you have the posters ready for display?"

"I think we need a picture of a couple from here to put on the poster. I would like to suggest Gordon and Marie," Celeste offered. "Harvey, I'm assuming that Harry will be willing to take the photo."

"Oh, that's for sure. I can have the posters done by Friday. I will also have fliers that we can place at everyone's door. I'll bring some ideas for decorations to the next meeting," Harvey said. "I think this is going to be fun."

"I've never been to a prom and I surely didn't date much when I was young. I was always working on the dairy farm," Frank said rather timidly.

"I'm sure you'll enjoy it, Frank. And, it will be another way for you to meet and mingle with other residents." Marty encouraged.

"I agree with Marty," Celeste said. "Let your male friends know that the women will be delighted to receive an invitation to go to the prom."

As the committee members were leaving the meeting, Frank hung back. When he was the only one still remaining in Marty's apartment, he turned to face her and said, "Marty, it's okay if you say *no*."

"To what?" she asked.

"To going to the prom with me."

Chapter 18

Rosebud and Ellie May were eagerly awaiting Marty's arrival. As the two of them sat at the table in Rosebud's kitchen, they kept watching the clock. Marty had told them that she expected the prom committee meeting to be over by three and it was already close to four.

"She should be here any minute now," Ellie May said as she tried to remain patient.

"I know that Susan is a no-good woman—I know it. She surely cannot afford to live in Kensington Place on her own," Rosebud stated firmly.

Just then the apartment door opened and Marty hurried in. "Sorry. The meeting went much longer than I had anticipated. And, have I got news for you," she said excitedly. "I have a date."

Rosebud looked startled. "A date? Who? When?" Rosebud said rapidly.

"Frank, the prom and the last Saturday in June," Marty fired back as she smiled.

Ellie May and Rosebud looked at one another for a few seconds.

"Is it that hard to believe that a man would ask me for a date? Am I that ugly?" Marty asked.

"Oh, Marty, no, no. I didn't know that Frank was...well, you know..."

"Is the word you're looking for *crazy*?" Marty asked as she laughed.

"When did all this happen?" Ellie May asked excitedly.

"During the meeting, Frank asked if only couples could come to the prom. We explained that anyone could come, but, if any of the men wanted to ask a lady to the prom, that would be nice. And, after the others had left the meeting, Frank asked me if he could take me to the prom," Marty giggled. "I was really surprised It's been a long time since anyone asked *me* for a date."

"I'm assuming that you said *yes*," Rosebud said. "Now, for sure, we must get you a really special gown for the affair. You need to give Abigail a run for her money," Rosebud said as she clapped her hands. "Oh, this is exciting."

"Okay, you two. If you're finished talking about the prom, can we get started on what we thought about Susan?" Ellie May asked impatiently.

"Me first." Rosebud said excitedly. "She's definitely Fredrick's mistress and…"

"Are you certain?" Marty asked.

"You bet I am. But, remember, she could also be a thief. I recommend that we begin to investigate the maintenance man, but keep our eye on Susan at the same time. She's moving to Kensington Place very quickly…like how can she afford that?" Rosebud stated.

"I agree that she's acting like someone who has a great deal of money. If that necklace was real, and if Susan took it and sold it, how much do you think she got?" Ellie May asked.

"From the description that you gave me, Marty, and if they were real diamonds, she could have gotten anywhere up to three-hundred thousand, but I can't be certain of that since I never had an opportunity to examine it," Rosebud explained. "If it was a really good imitation, then perhaps two to three thousand."

"I see," Ellie May said. "It looks as if we must update our plans. How do we proceed from here?"

"The only other person that was in my apartment was Preston, the maintenance man. But he has a pristine reputation—it just cannot be him," Marty stated.

"What do you know about his personal life that makes you say he has a pristine reputation?" Rosebud asked.

"Hortense told me that and she should know. After all, she's the one who hired him," Marty argued.

"I once belonged to a church where the minister ran away with the organist and they never came back. At one time, they too had pristine reputations!" argued Ellie May.

"Tell you what. I'll ask Preston to change my bathroom light fixture. I'll engage him in some idle conversation and then I'll get back to you both," Rosebud said.

"I don't know much about pawn shops, but could Susan have pawned the necklace?" Ellie May asked.

Marty thought about that possibility. "Hmmm—a pawn shop. If she pawned it, that would mean she got a loan…she could have done that; she could have done that; but, if she sold it outright, she would have gotten much more. Perhaps we should visit the two pawn shops we have in town…but, then again, if she sold it, she probably took it out of town where people wouldn't know her…but, if she sold it privately, we might never find out who bought it and how much they paid for it."

"Oh, let's go to the pawn shops. That sounds so mysterious—you know—like we are hoods," Ellie May begged.

"Crooks!" Rosebud almost shouted. "Ellie May, you watch far too many crime shows. Next thing you know, you'll want us to become bikers and wear leather jackets."

"If it helps keep Marty out of jail, then we'll do that, too," Ellie May said.

"I guess you'll also want us to pack?" Rosebud teased.

"I know what that means. No, I don't think we need to carry guns," Ellie May said.

"But, you could keep your gun in your apron pocket, Ellie May," Rosebud said as she broke out in laughter.

"Let's get back to being serious," Marty suggested. "Rosebud, you try talking with Preston. See what your instincts are about his honesty. But, I will bet you a hundred dollars that he had absolutely nothing to do with my missing necklace."

"Right now, I believe that Susan took it. Anyone who goes after a married man cannot be trusted at all. She's a hussy," Rosebud said.

"Can we go to the pawn shop tomorrow, Marty?" Ellie May asked. "We can't let the trail get cold. Oh, oh, can't we get someone in to look for DNA on your doll cabinet? DNA doesn't lie, but mistresses do."

"Ellie May, how can we do that when we can't tell anyone about the necklace?" Rosebud said sharply.

"Right now, I wish that I had never found that damned thing," Marty said. "Look at all the trouble it's causing."

"I'm sorry someone took it, Marty, but all this is so exciting. There's no one else in this whole place who's having such fun. I have lived such a boring life—this has renewed me. Now, again, can we go to the pawn shops tomorrow?" Ellie May pleaded. "Please say *yes*."

Chapter 19

Ellie May was so excited she could hardly contain herself. She always had thought of pawn shops as places where criminals went to sell their ill-gotten gains. The fact that several people were strolling around the *Last Chance Pawn Shop* surprised her. She had envisioned that the place would be dark and dreary—almost like a store that really didn't want anyone to enter. One woman was peering in a case that was filled with all brands of watches, while her friend seemed to be more interested in the art work that lined the walls. Ellie May could not understand why such normal-looking people would shop in a place like this. While the store was really brightly-lit and sparkling clean, Ellie May wasn't feeling that way about the merchandise that was for sale. She wondered how many of these things had been in the hands of criminals not too long ago.

"May I help you," the clerk behind the counter asked Ellie May.

"I'm here with my two friends," she answered, pointing to Marty and Rosebud.

The clerk turned to Marty and asked, "How may I be of service to you?"

"I'm looking for something dramatic—preferably something with diamonds. My granddaughter is getting married and she would like something that would look amazing with her strapless gown," Marty explained. "What I see in this case is not suitable. Would you by chance have other, more elegant pieces, that you could show me?"

"We normally do not deal in high-priced diamonds since most of our customers prefer something less costly. However, the shop across town may be able to help you. I encourage you to look over our selection very carefully. We have several pieces from a private collection that are absolutely divine," the clerk said as he slowly removed a velvet-lined tray from the case.

"Oh, Marty," Rosebud said. "Look at that necklace—exquisite."

"I agree, but my little darling wants diamonds. Thank you for your help," she said to the clerk. "Come, we need to move on."

As they climbed into Marty's car, Rosebud said, "I really liked that necklace. I almost forgot why we were there," she giggled.

Before too long, they were walking into *Fred's Fine Finds Pawn Shop*. As they entered the store, Marty said, "I don't believe it. Look, there's Susan."

At that moment, Rosebud and Ellie May almost bumped into one another trying to get a glimpse of their prime suspect. Susan was talking with one of the clerks, while holding slips of paper in her hand. When she spied Marty, she turned and waved. When she finished her transaction, she approached Marty and extended her hand.

"Mrs. Miller, how nice to see you again," Susan said warmly. "I was finally able to pick up some items that I had loans on here. Now that I am making a decent wage, I'm finally able to live more comfortably. They have some remarkable buys here, Mrs. Miller. I saw an especially chic string of pearls in the second case up front. You may want to take a look at them before you leave. I know how much you love pearls."

"I may do that, Susan," Marty replied.

After Susan left the shop, the three of them huddled. "Wow, was that a coincidence, or what?" Rosebud said. "Maybe you might find your necklace right here."

Marty walked over to the clerk. "I'm looking for a necklace for my granddaughter who is getting married. She would like something in diamonds that would set off her strapless wedding gown in an elegant fashion. I was going to go directly to *Jared's,* but a friend of mine recommended that I check with you first," Marty lied agreeably.

"Let me show you what I have. I'll be right back," he said.

Rosebud whispered, "Marty, I think we're going to see your necklace."

When the clerk returned, he gently placed a three strand diamond necklace in front of Marty. "Isn't this a dramatic piece?"

Marty's expectations were dashed. It was not her necklace. "I really wanted something with more strands," she said in an obviously disappointed tone.

"This is the only diamond necklace we have at the moment."

"The lady you were helping earlier was a friend of mine. She said that she was reclaiming items on which she had obtained loans. Did she by chance sell you a diamond necklace?" Marty questioned.

"I'm not at liberty to respond to that question. I'm sorry, but all our loans and sales are confidential. I'm certain that you can understand that," the clerk explained.

"Certainly. She had a necklace at one time that I truly admired, and I was hoping that she might have sold it to you. I apologize. Thank you for your help."

As they drove out the parking lot, Rosebud said, "Bummer. I thought that we had found it. But the fact that she was there, reclaiming items, only proves that she is totally familiar with pawn shops. I still think she's our target."

Chapter 20

"Daddy, you're going where?" Frank's oldest daughter asked in an unbelievable tone.

"To a prom."

"What kind of prom?"

"Just a prom. Some of the residents thought that it would be fun to have a prom, and since I have never had an opportunity to go dancing, let alone a prom—I thought I would see what the world of fun looks like," Frank said, as he faced his four daughters. When none of them responded, he said, "Well, now you know why you need to teach me how to dance."

Cora, Lucy, June, and Delores were all smiles. "Dad," Delores said "we never would have imagined that you would want to dance—you know—that was not very thoughtful of us. You were always so busy with the dairy farm, and taking care of us that we made an assumption that you just weren't interested in a social life. And, Dad, I can't get over that you're taking someone to the prom," June said in amazement.

"She's a nice lady," Frank said resolutely.

"I'm certain of that," Delores said. "No one deserves to have some fun more than you, Dad. We've got to make certain that you have the right clothes to wear. And, don't forget, you must find out what color she will be wearing so you can purchase an appropriate corsage. She might want an arm corsage, or maybe…"

"Now, wait a minute, girls. This is a lot for me to remember. Marty is a fine-looking woman and…"

Frank's daughters started laughing. In a deep voice, Cora said, "'A fine-looking woman?' Dad, people don't talk like that anymore. Is she *hot*?"

"Cora! Don't be disrespectful!" Frank chided.

"No, Dad, that just means, well, you know, whistle bait."

"Oh, where did I go wrong with you girls? Marty is a nice-looking woman—an upstanding woman," Frank tried to explain.

"I can't wait to meet this Marty. Does she realize how lucky she is to be to be going to a prom with our handsome father? You're only the best-looking man in this whole place," Cora said convincingly.

"Dad, do you still have your record player?" Lucy asked.

"Sure do," Frank replied.

"Well, let's get started with your dancing lessons. After all, we want to be certain that you'll actually dance and not just sit at a table all night. Remember, you cannot treat your date like a wallflower," Lucy said lovingly.

In just a few minutes, Frank had placed his record player on the table, moved a few chairs, and was standing in the center of the room with his arms wide open. As Lucy moved towards her father, Delores, said, "You take charge of the lessons, I'll go check Dad's wardrobe to see what he'll need for the prom."

As the Frank Sinatra songs spewed forth from the old record player, Lucy tenderly began instructing her dad. Lucy could not stop smiling. She was seeing a different side of her father. Their mother had died a slow, painful death from cancer when the youngest was only three, but the girls had never wanted for anything. Their dad had learned how to braid their hair, iron ruffled dresses, and, along with their beloved Aunt Nina, had provided love and guidance as they had moved through high school, college, and marriages.

Snyder's Dairy Farm had grown to be the largest dairy operation in southeastern Pennsylvania. And, when Frank had finally sold the farm, he had given a generous gift to each of his daughters. Lucy recalled the day that they all sat in the lawyer's office as their dad had proudly shared his financial dealings with them. When they had argued that he should keep his money since he might need it at a later date, he said, "Girls, look, please use the money I have given you as you see fit. It's up to you. But, I hope to see you enjoy whatever you do with it."

"It's my turn," Cora said, as she tapped her sister on the shoulder. After they had been dancing for a few minutes, June said, "I'm next."

When Delores came back into the living room, she said, "Dad, you have a gorgeous black suit that will be fine for the prom. Find out what

Marty will be wearing, and then choose a bow tie that will match her gown."

"Dad, what's Marty's last name? When we meet her, we can't call her Marty," Delores stated.

"*Miller.* Her last name is *Miller.* I'm pleased to see that you girls still have some manners," Frank said with a broad smile.

"This is so exciting. On the night of the prom, Dad, will it be alright for me to come and take pictures of Marty and you?" Delores asked.

"Well, yes, but don't hang around too long. After all, this will be the first date that I have had in more than fifty years," he said as he hugged Delores.

June then turned to her dad, and said, "Daddy, is it possible that we girls might finally be getting a new Mommie?"

Chapter 21

Marie Turnbull was busy helping several ladies from Morning Glory Hill as they looked through the racks and racks of clothes on their hunt for something special to wear to the prom. She felt that this might possibly be one of her last duties as the owner of *Marie's Closet*. While she had promised her husband that she would close the shop, she was now having second thoughts about being away from her little corner of the fashion world. While Gordon would still be serving on several boards, requiring blocks of his time, if she gave up her shop, she didn't know how she would fill her days. She had received only one offer for the shop so far, but it was certainly not acceptable. Perhaps she could convince Gordon that she needed to stay in business until she received a decent offer.

"Ladies, in the side room you'll find some of the newest fashions from the *House of London*. These include ankle-length dresses and skirts. And, to the left are at least a dozen, amazing, beaded bags on display that would be perfect for the prom," Marie said as she moved gracefully among the customers.

"Marie," Rosebud said, "I'm looking for something form-fitting without any ruffles or girly stuff—know what I mean?"

"Oh, Rosebud, I've already put something away for you. Wait till you see it," Marie said excitedly as she hurried to the back room. When she returned, Rosebud's eyes opened wide as she saw the sparkling silver creation that demanded her attention.

Looking at the tag, Rosebud noted that it was her size. "How did you know?" Rosebud asked as she took the hanger out of Marie's hand, immediately disappearing into a dressing room.

When Rosebud reappeared, all heads turned—something Rosebud didn't fail to notice. As she spun around in her gown, Rosebud couldn't have asked for anything more. The metallic silver gown was soft to the touch. The long sleeves were sheer silver chiffon, while the trumpet- –shaped skirt hugged her slim figure perfectly. She kept twirling around to admire herself. The way that the fabric moved gave the illusion that she had nothing on underneath. She hadn't felt this sexy in many, many years. Her search for a gown that would make her stand out at the prom was over—this shiny, silvery creation was perfect.

"Rosebud, it looks as if it was tailored just for you," Marty said. "It's stunning."

"My goodness. That is a gorgeous gown," Ellie May said. "This is so much fun, isn't it? I can hardly imagine that I am excited about shopping—at my age!"

"Marie, I'll take it; that's for sure. I just love everything about it," Rosebud said as she openly admired herself in the three-way mirror.

"You have the figure to wear that gown," Marie said wholeheartedly.

"Rosebud, if you're not voted Prom Queen, I can't imagine who would be," Ellie May declared.

"And, you must have at least six or seven pairs of sandals that would look amazing," Marty teased. "Now, stop admiring yourself in the mirror and come and help Ellie May and me pick our gowns."

"Marty, you surely don't need me to help you with your selection," Ellie May said.

"I surely do. It's always best to get a second opinion. After all, we are good friends and I know that you will let me know how I really look in something," Marty said. "Let's look over the ankle-length skirts that Marie mentioned. I always wanted something from *The House of London*. These prints are gorgeous. You know, Ellie May, when I go to the prom, it will be my first date in many years. I want to look my best."

Marty thought that the prints were magnificent and the solid-colored garments were the latest shades. This could possibly take her all day to choose just one. Secretly, she had been worried about what she should wear on her first date in umpteen years. Frank had seemed to avoid her since he had asked her to go to the dance. She rationalized that this was just a sign of his nervousness. After all, he had been a widower since his daughters were quite young. Marty had been amazed how often she had thought about the day that Frank stood before her saying that it was alright if she said *no*. She seemed to have lost some of her eagerness to locate her necklace, but she hadn't mentioned this to her friends. Rosebud would probably give her a lecture about how valuable that piece of jewelry might be and would warn her about making too much out of *this Frank thing.*

As she perused the last rack of skirts, she found a pure silk creation in the most fetching shade of lilac that she had ever seen. When she ran her fingers over the material, it was like touching air—if there was such a thing. She draped the skirt over her arm and began examining the jackets and tops that were on display on the next rack. Ellie May also was looking through the rack. Suddenly, Ellie May spied a lace jacket with long sheer sleeves. Around the neckline, and spilling down the front of the jacket, dark purple beads formed tiny little flowers—pretty without being gaudy; in other words, in good taste.

"Marty, I may have found it," Ellie May said proudly, as she held the jacket up for Marty to examine.

"Ellie, it's perfect!" As Marty held the jacket against the skirt, Ellie May beamed.

"How are you doing, Marty?" Marie asked as she popped her head around the corner.

"Ellie May found it, Marie, and I love the combination of this skirt and the matching jacket."

As Marie took the hangers out of Marty's hand, she said, "Here, Marty, let me take you over to the dressing room. Meanwhile, Ellie May and I will start on our hunt for her special outfit."

Ellie May was not a bit comfortable in this fancy dress shop on her own. She was not accustomed to looking at fabrics and colors. Her entire wardrobe consisted of practical things, so she didn't know anything about gowns and such. Aimlessly, she looked over a rack of gowns. The bright colors were something she was not used to. She held up a pink chiffon dress with three-quarter sleeves and a jewel neckline. While she thought it was pretty, she knew that it was much too young-looking for her. Next, she examined a blue silk dress, but when she saw that it was sleeveless, she immediately put it back on the rack.

"I might have to change my mind about going to the prom. I guess I'm just not cut out for things like this," Ellie May said despondently.

"I have something that I think you may like," Marie said as she went around the other side of the rack. "Here it is," Marie said happily.

Ellie May was pleased when she saw that the ice blue, silk chiffon dress had long sleeves and a small scoop neckline. A jeweled cummerbund at the waist held tiny pleats in place. "I'm willing to try that on," Ellie May said.

Feeling very awkward, Ellie May made certain that no one was watching her as she twisted and turned to examine herself in the well-lit mirror. She was surprised when she realized she liked what she saw. Blue was definitely her color. She ran her hands over the cummerbund and was surprised that she could actually feel her waist—a part of her body that was usually covered with a white apron. Suddenly, she felt years younger. It would be nice if her husband could see her now. While he had told her often that she was beautiful, she never believed him. She thought of herself as plain and ordinary. But, in this gown, she certainly didn't feel ordinary. She blushed when she saw Marty and Rosebud heading her way.

"Ellie May, you look fabulous!" Rosebud said excitedly. "You need to buy that outfit no matter what it costs," Rosebud said.

"I agree," Marty said.

When the three friends finally left *Marie's Closet*, they were all smiles. "Looks like we hit the jackpot," Marty said. "I really enjoyed this venture. Shopping with you two is such a joy. When the fall items are in the store, we must come back again," Marty chuckled. As they carefully placed their prom dresses in the trunk of Marty's car, they were as excited as teen-agers.

"Isn't that Marie something else? She seems to know us better than we know ourselves," Rosebud said. "But that's a sign of a good business owner. I only hope someone that astute will be the next owner. Wait a minute—what if we three form a company and we buy *Marie's Closet?*"

"Rosebud, we're all too old to begin a venture like that," Marty argued.

"I guess you're right. But it would've been fun, don't you think?" Rosebud responded. As she settled in the passenger seat, she said, "Drive carefully, Marty. I've got the sexiest gown that I have ever seen stored in your trunk and, at my age, I probably will never find another one like it, so no rear-end collisions, or my lawyer will be calling your lawyer."

Chapter 22

It was midnight and the only two patrons in *The Night Owl* were William and Nigel. Stretch had made a brief appearance, but he had to hurry back to the kitchen since he needed to make bread and sweet rolls for the breakfast crowd. Nigel was aimlessly stirring his hot chocolate, making sure that he scraped all the whipped cream from the sides of the mug.

"Well, I guess I'll go to the prom—just to irritate some people," Nigel said in a grumpy tone.

"If you don't want to go, don't. It's just that easy, Nigel. I encouraged you to ask one of the ladies to go with you, but you are so damned stubborn, you won't do that," William said.

"I can have fun all by myself," Nigel said firmly.

"And then you can dance all by yourself," William argued.

Nigel just kept stirring his hot choclate until William reached across the table and placed his hand on Nigel's arm. "You know, Frank is taking Marty," William said. "Why don't you ask Rosebud?"

"She hates me."

"Now, how do you know that?" William questioned.

"I can tell. She, well, she sort of wrinkles up her nose when I talk to her. She's too snooty for me," Nigel added grumpily.

"Well, how about Celeste, or Ellie May, or Sally? They're all nice women."

"Let me tell you why not: Sally's too fat, Celeste always has her nose in a book, and Ellie May—well, she looks like a housewife."

"Oh, and you are Brad Pitt or something?" William chuckled.

"I think I'm okay. Brad Pitt? No, not quite, but close," Nigel said as he laughed.

"You are hopeless," William said with a sigh. "Go to the prom. I'm sure that you'll find someone you can dance with. Oh, here comes

Jessie. I forgot to mention her," William said as he pulled up a chair for the new arrival.

"Good evening, gentlemen," Jessie said. "So, we meet again at *The Night Owl*. You know, they say *birds of a feather flock together.*"

"Cut me a break," Nigel said in an irritated tone. "Must you always rhyme?"

"No, Mr. Grumpy Bear, I do not have to rhyme all the time. But when I feel like it, I do."

"I guess she told you, Nigel," William said as he smiled. "Jessie, are you going to the prom?"

"Yes, I am. Four of the ladies on Marigold are going together. You better watch out, Nigel. Those women may have their eyes on you. You never can tell," Jessie teased as she winked at William.

"Well, no wonder. I'm a fine specimen of an available bachelor," Nigel bragged.

"Jessie, did you ever go to the *Rainbow Dance Hall* at the old amusement park? Back in the 40s and 50s, big bands, like Duke Ellington, used to play there," William said.

"I did, William. I used to sneak out of the house, get on the trolley car, and ride to the park. I'd work my way up to the stage as close as I could so I could see their faces. Once in a while, someone would ask me to dance and that would really make my night," Jessie said as she allowed herself to sway back and forth in her chair.

"I had a '37 Ford, but I couldn't always use it during the 40s because gas was rationed then," William said.

"I have a funny story to tell you about gas rationing. I graduated from high school in '45 and gas was still being rationed. So, a group of six of us figured that if we all went in one car, we could pool our ration stamps and drive to the prom. Well, we three girls were wearing gowns that had yards and yards of netting in the skirts. We squeezed ourselves in the back and our dates—all outfitted in white sport coats—sat in the front. All was well until we were on our way home," Jessie began laughing. "Driving through a powerful thunder storm, we ran out of gas."

"That was a dumb thing to do, Nigel said.

"We thought so, too. The boys decided that they would push the car. They told me to hop up front and steer the car. Here I was, up to my chin in netting, trying to climb over and get into the front seat. Miraculously, a car stopped and the driver took us all home," Jessie said as she banged her cane on the floor.

"No time for any hanky-panky?" Nigel asked.

"Nigel, for heaven's sake, you owe Jessie any apology," William insisted.

"Never mind that, William, I'm used to his stupid remarks." Jessie replied.

"I hear that we'll have quite a full house for the prom," Jessie said. "Marty told me that they have over a hundred reservations. I've been exercising on a daily basis, so maybe I'll be able to complete at least a dance or two without the use of my cane."

"Will you save one for me?" William asked.

"Why, I'd be delighted," Jessie replied, happily. "I know at least two ladies who have their caps set for you," Jessie teased.

William looked at Nigel in disbelief—he was blushing and he had no retort for Jessie.

The kitchen door popped open and Stretch appeared with a tray of goodies. "You folks want a taste?"

"I don't think Nigel wants any," Jessie said thoughtfully. "*Nigel, Nigel, did you know, that our women are aglow, at the thought of getting a date, and making you their newest mate?*"

Chapter 23

Morning Glory Hill was a bed of activity. It was the day of *The Senior Prom* and, no matter where one looked, something was occurring that involved this special occasion. The beauty salon was filled to capacity. Two additional hairdressers had been hired to help with the overflow. And, the *Crown Beauty School* had provided three students to give manicures and polish nails. As fast as one lady left the chair, another took her place. The ladies were enjoying the hubbub as they shared details of what they would be wearing that evening.

"I'm more excited about this prom than I was about my senior prom in high school," Rosebud mused as she kept a careful eye on the young woman, who was using the curling iron on her hair. "I just hope that the men who are coming won't just sit on their butts. I really want to dance. My legs feel really good and I want to enjoy this evening."

"When they get a look at you in that dress," Marty said, "we'll have to use a baseball bat to keep them away from you."

"You should talk," Rosebud said. "I saw you in that lilac outfit—spectacular! Did you tell Frank what color you're wearing? I hope he doesn't bring a red rose or some other flower that clashes," Rosebud stated.

Quietly, Marty whispered in Rosebud's ear, "His daughter called me."

"Get out of here," Rosebud replied.

"I saw a *Schmehl's Flowers* delivery truck just a few minutes ago," Marty said. "They carried in several large bouquets that I believe will be in the dining room. It's going to be a spectacular night. Ladies, I'll see you all later," she said as she waved goodbye over her shoulder.

As she walked across The Square, Marty was surprised to see Frank headed her way. "Marty, I need to apologize to you. My daughter told me that she checked with you about the color of your gown."

"No need to apologize, Frank. I thought it was very sweet of her to call," Marty reassured Frank.

"Well, she knows that I don't know much about these kinds of things. But she should have told me to call you. However, I have a favor to ask. My girls want to take our picture tonight when I pick you up—that is, if it's okay with you."

"Of course," Marty said. "It'll be a nice memento for both of us."

"What time should l pick you up, Marty?"

"I think quarter of six would be fine, Frank."

She watched as Frank hurried over to the reception desk, where she could see several corsage boxes stacked up in one corner. She moved behind a pillar. From her hiding spot, Marty could watch Frank. She spied Mary Beth handing him a box. Frank hurried away, trying not to let anyone see what he was carrying.

Away from the excited crowd, three men were erecting a trellis around the doorway to the dining room. Woven throughout the trellis, a profusion of blue, pink, and white morning glories bloomed lavishly. As soon as the trellis was fastened, the men hurried inside the dining room and closed the doors behind them.

Barry began instructing the men on how to position the tables and chairs. Using a seating chart that Harvey Hamilton had made, Barry followed them around the room, checking and double-checking their work. He was surprised when Mary Beth tapped his shoulder.

"Barry, the entry is gorgeous. Nothing could focus on the theme better than that trellis covered with morning glories. Our residents will love it. I'm here to help. Do you want me to begin setting the tables?" she inquired as she pulled a metal cart behind her.

"Yes. Here's a copy of Harvey's plan. If you find any errors, give me a whistle. The florist will be arriving in just a few minutes with the table centerpieces. They must be handled gently since the flowers are in glass bowls that have water in them," Barry said as he headed for the stage area.

As Mary Beth began her work with a flourish, Hortense appeared. "Need help?" she asked.

"Sure. I'll take care of the table covers and the napkins. You can put the table numbers and the place cards on each table. Here's the sketch.

We need to be certain that we have the right guests at the right tables. We don't want to start World War III," Mary Beth joked.

"Who made these beautiful place cards?' Hortense asked.

"Harvey did. Can't you tell? That man is so talented," Mary Beth replied.

Just as Mary Beth and Hortense were working on the last two tables, the florist arrived with the centerpieces.

"Aren't these precious?" Mary Beth said.

"This brings back memories of how this property looked before they built our facility," Hortense said. "Morning glories climbed the trees and lay in patches of riotous color all over the ground. It makes me feel warm all over to see all these morning glories in full bloom."

Before too long, the silverware was placed on the tables by workers using twelve-inch rulers to make sure that the space needed for the appetizers would be available for the wait staff. Then, two young servers placed champagne glasses on the tables.

Barry stood in the center of the room, admiring the site. The room looked as elegant as any he remembered from the dining salons on the cruise ships. Just then the back door opened, and the delivery man from the *Mount Sunshine Playhouse* waved to him. Barry hurried to greet him. He couldn't wait to see how the thrones would actually look close up. When he lifted the dust cloths, he was pleased. The reproductions looked very authentic with the gold edging and dark red velvet seats. Barry had been delighted when the playhouse had agreed to lend them for the prom. He now concluded that the prom king and queen would look very royal, indeed, especially since the theater also had sent along crowns for the royal couple.

Barry then turned his attention to the stage. He took charge as the men moved chairs and positioned the piano for *The Melody Makers*, the six-piece orchestra that would provide the music for dancing. As Barry was creating a special spot for the harpist, who would be playing as guests arrived as well as during dinner, Harvey rushed in. "My goodness, Barry, you're just about finished in here. Sorry I'm late."

"The sketches you created did the trick. Look around to make certain that we interpreted your drawings correctly. Look at this place,

Harvey. You thought of everything. You did an amazing job. How do you like the thrones for the king and queen?"

"Perfect, Barry, absolutely perfect. I'm glad that you kept the doors closed. I want the guests to be surprised as they step into the doorway tonight," Harvey said. "Were you able to get judges?"

"Sure did—the director of the playhouse and two actors, who are from out of town. So, no one has any ties with the people here. It just removes any bias when they have to select the king and queen."

Six hours later, The Square came to life again. Two of Frank's daughters arrived and they went immediately to Lilac Lane and sat on a bench near Marty's apartment. Before too long, they spied their dad coming down the hall. They were amazed. He looked impeccable in his dark suit and lilac bow tie. His shoes shone with each step he took. He tried to pretend that he didn't see the girls, but he couldn't help smiling. He rang Marty's doorbell.

When the door opened, and Frank got his first look at Marty in her formal gown, he was awe-struck. He thought she was beautiful before; but tonight—well, tonight, she was breathtaking. He opened his mouth to speak, but nothing came out.

"Hello, Frank. My, don't you look handsome," Marty said as she smiled broadly.

"Hello, Marty. You sure look pretty," he said rather awkwardly.

"Mrs. Miller," Delores said as she peeked around her dad. "Excuse me, we would like to take some pictures."

"Certainly, let me get my bag," Marty said as she reached into her apartment to retrieve her beaded bag.

"Dad, I'll take a picture as you give Marty her orchid," June said.

Frank moved towards Marty, and with shaking hands, he handed her the orchid.

"Pin it on her gown," Delores directed.

Frank was really nervous now. He held the orchid in one hand and the corsage pin in the other. "Marty, I hope I don't hurt you," he said.

"Tell you what. I'll hold my lapel out for you, Frank. You won't hurt me," Marty reassured him. As he nervously handled the orchid, Marty said, "Thank you, Frank. It's been a long, long time since I have had an orchid—it's beautiful."

With the corsage in place, Frank stood alongside Marty, slid his arm around her waist and smiled. After his daughters took several shots, he said, "Okay, girls. You know the prom is tonight. I think Marty and I are old enough to get ourselves there."

Marty took Frank's arm and they walked down the hall, across The Square and toward the dining room. When they reached the entranceway, Marty said, "Frank, look, isn't this colorful? The morning glories are magnificent."

Mary Beth was seated at a table near the doorway. She greeted each guest and directed them to their numbered table. As the dining room became alive, the harpist began playing. Shortly, the room was filled with men and women in formal wear. The overhead lights had been dimmed, creating an atmosphere as close as possible to candlelight. Harvey had wanted to have candles on each table, but open-flame candles were forbidden in Morning Glory Hill, so he begrudgingly settled for dimmers.

Marty and Frank were seated at a table near the stage. "Isn't it nice to have a harpist here, Frank? It's hard to believe that this is our regular dining room. Look at the thrones they have for the Prom King and Queen," Marty said as she laughed.

"I must say, Marty, you are the prettiest lady here tonight," Frank said hesitantly.

"How nice of you to say that, Frank."

"I think you should be the queen," he said softly.

"Go on, Frank. I really doubt that will happen," she said as she smiled at him.

After the champagne glasses had been filled, Barry picked up the mike.

"Ladies and gentlemen, let's raise our glasses to one another. Here's to good friends and fellowship that we all enjoy. May we meet like this for many years to come."

After dinner, the wait staff cleared the tables with speed just as the orchestra began playing. "Marty, would you like to dance? I'm not too good, yet, but I would love to dance with you," Frank said shyly.

Marty and Frank were the first two on the dance floor. Marty was pleasantly surprised at how well Frank maneuvered her around the floor.

She was grateful, however, when she realized that several other couples, including William and Abigail, were also dancing. After several pieces, Barry approached the microphone.

"Welcome, folks. I hope you all enjoyed your dinner," he said. The room burst into applause and Barry shook his head in agreement.

"I hope you're ready for some fun. Mary Beth will be moving about, handing out envelopes to a dozen men. Gentlemen, please do not open them before I tell you to. If you are chosen, please bring your envelope with you as you come to the center of the dance floor."

Mary Beth was an expert at getting the men to participate. Before too long, she had twelve apprehensive men standing in a line.

"Now, ladies, it's your time to get involved. Look at these handsome men very carefully. Without causing any fist fights, you will have the pleasure of dancing with one of Morning Glory Hills' most handsome men. Now, Mary Beth will chose a dozen ladies. You too will get an envelope."

As soon as the ladies were chosen, Barry said, "Ladies you may open your envelopes. Now, gentlemen, open your envelopes and hold your number in front of you. Okay, ladies, go get the man who's holding the number you have."

The room instantly filled with laughter. Soon the ladies were paired with their partners and the music began. Marty was surprised to see that Rosebud had been matched up with Nigel—someone she really didn't like. But she was a good sport and put her hand on Nigel's shoulder, ready to dance. Much to everyone's surprise, Nigel swept her away as he demonstrated to everyone that he was a fantastic dancer. As the music played, Nigel and Rosebud danced gracefully around the dance floor. He held her at arm's length, and it was as if his feet didn't even have to touch the floor. Despite his girth, he moved as lightly as a feather. Rosebud seemed to be mesmerized. When the music stopped, the guests all stood up and applauded. As Nigel escorted Rosebud back to her table properly, people along the way congratulated them. Rosebud was speechless.

Once again, Barry approached the microphone. "Ladies and gentlemen, I would like to introduce some special guests: Mr. Jason Simpson, Director of the *Mount Sunshine Playhouse*; and Miss Greta

Von Horton and Mr. Gregory Updike, from our local playhouse, are our judges for the selection of Prom King and Queen. The judges tell me that they have been making copious notes ever since you arrived, but they pledge to narrow their choices down before the clock strikes eight."

Across the dining room the chatter level rose to a new height. Some guests were already predicting who would be chosen. When the orchestra began to play a Cha Cha Cha, only a few couples were brave enough to work their way to the dance floor. When the guests spotted Rosebud and Nigel in the center of the dance floor, there was a burst of applause. The couple did not disappoint their admirers. Rosebud beamed and Nigel's smile could not have been broader. Nigel certainly owned the dance floor and he knew it. When he touched Rosebud, it was as if he were afraid that she would break. It was obvious that Rosebud was enjoying her new notoriety.

At eight, Barry crossed the stage with the crowns on a velvet pillow. "Folks, it's time that we honor our king and queen. Mr. Simpson, will you please make the official announcement?"

Clearing his throat, Simpson said, "It gives me great pleasure to introduce you to your Prom King, Mr. Nigel Nugget. Mr. Nugget, please join us here on the stage."

Greta Von Horton then placed the crown on Nigel's head. "I now dub you Prom King of Morning Glory Hill, 2016."

The crowd responded with hoots and hollers. They stood up and welcomed their new king with applause.

"Of course, every king must have a queen," Simpson said. "Will Rosebud McClaren join us on the stage?"

When Nigel had been declared king, Rosebud had secretly crossed her fingers, hoping that she would be chosen queen. She hurried across the dance floor. As she mounted the steps, Updike took her hand and led her to the mike. "I dub you Prom Queen of Morning Glory Hill, 2016."

Nigel moved close to Rosebud and took her hand. He led her to her throne and gallantly bowed to her as she sat down—the crowd went wild.

The evening seemed to fly by. After the royal dance, the orchestra played a variety of music and, with each song, the dance floor grew more crowded. Barry got the crowd to participate in the *Chicken Dance*, and even the *Electric Slide*. While there were more ladies present than gentlemen, even they paired off and enjoyed just being out on the dance floor.

With the playing of *Goodnight Sweetheart*, the guests realized that their prom was coming to an end. As they filed out of the dining room, the air was filled with lighthearted voices and a sense of euphoria.

When Frank and Marty reached The Square, he turned to her and said, "Marty, thank you so much for allowing me to take you to the prom. It was a great evening. I'm sorry that it is over."

"I have an idea, Frank—suppose we just go for a walk. It's such a gorgeous evening so perhaps we can go out to the gazebo and just talk—that is, if you're not too tired."

"Let me hold your hand, Marty. I don't want you to fall." Frank took her hand and led her out the front entrance. They walked down the sidewalk, following the pathway to the little gazebo that was bathed in moonlight. As they sat down, Frank said softly, "Marty, look. The sky is filled with millions of stars. It must be an omen."

Chapter 24

As Marty sat with Frank in the little gazebo at Morning Glory Hill, she was totally unaware that across town at *Serenity,* an episode was unfolding that would shake the whole town. An old, Ford Falcon sedan had rolled up in front of the posh restaurant, depositing Sadie and Mabel, the night cleaning crew, who headed for the front door, wearing long, cotton skirts and orthopedic shoes, they resembled the char women from the *Carol Burnett Show.* Sadie pulled a key from her bra and opened the door, which she held open for Mable. She was proud that Mr. Fredrick, the owner, had given her the key because, in her eyes, it put her up one rung on the ladder above Mable.

"Since Mr. Fredrick's car is in the parking lot, we don't have to clean his office so we'll get finished a little early tonight," Sadie said as she opened the closet door and began pulling out buckets and mops.

"Why does he come here and work so late at night?" Mabel asked. "If I owned such a ritzy place, I'd have workers do everything. Maybe it takes him that long to count all his money," she said as she laughed.

"I'm not sure, but I bet you dollars to doughnuts that he sometimes has women in there," Sadie stated. "Come on. Let's start tonight in the *Garden Room.*"

The two friends moved almost mechanically around the room, making sure that everything was spic-and-span. "You know, Sadie, I don't know how they keep these plants thriving like they do. As soon as I get a plant at home, I kill it. I either give it too much water or not enough."

"I know that there is a man who comes in and prunes them and feeds them with some kind of stuff that makes them grow. Okay, we're done in here. Let's head for the rest rooms next," Sadie said. "We need to put on our rubber aprons and gloves. That stuff we put in the toilets is wicked."

"I hate these ugly, yellow rubber things," Mabel complained.

"Hey, you want to get your skin eaten off? Put them on," Sadie ordered.

As they moved towards the restrooms, the strains of music began to fill the air. "I recognize that piece," Sadie said knowingly. "It's Ravel's *Bolero*. I can't imagine why Mr. Fredrick would play such music if he was working. I wonder…"

She motioned Mabel to follow her. Moving quietly down the hallway, she ducked into the kitchen and hurried into a storage area. Walking to the wall, she took hold of a small knob and pushed it to the side. An opening appeared, allowing them to look directly into the boss's office. Sadie motioned for Mabel to come closer and whispered, "The previous owner of this place used to have his dinners delivered this way to keep everyone out of his office."

When they looked through the window, they were instantly mesmerized. Sadie rubbed her eyes to make sure that she was really awake and that this was really happening. Fredrick and Susan were naked as jay birds and dancing around the room, enveloped in matching white feathered boas. As the dancing became more frenzied, feathers flew in all directions. The deep, passionate music of *Bolero* was having an effect on the two dancers as well as the two onlookers. Sadie and Mable were leaning on a table so they could get closer to the opening. They could not keep still. Their rear ends swayed back and forth in time with the sensual sounds of the clarinets, French horns, and flutes as each instrument assumed its rightful place in the melody.

Susan would occasionally wrap her feather boa around Fredrick and pull him closer and then, just as quickly, she would spin away. Fredrick's face said it all—he was spellbound. Naked, except for black knee stockings, he looked like a buffoon. Sadie thought he was the funniest-looking thing she had seen in a long time.

All of a sudden, their immersion in the whole scene was rattled when Fredrick's office door flew open to reveal an angry Cassandra, his wife. "Oh…my…God," whispered Sadie, "she's got a gun in her hand!"

Screaming like a banshee, Cassandra yelled, "You s.o.b. Prancing around like a half-wit with a two-bit whore. I should kill you both!"

"Shall I call 911?" a terrified Mabel whispered.

"Not yet. Let the old geezer stew in his juices a little while longer," replied Sadie. "With her poor eye sight, she probably couldn't hit the side of a barn door."

No sooner were the words out of her mouth when the gun went off. Sadie was scared, but then realized that Cassandra had missed Fredrick. Instead she had shot a hole in his prize photo of Vice-president Dick Cheney and him at a golf course. Susan was trying desperately to get to her clothes that were piled on a sofa behind Cassandra. It was time for Sadie to call 911—she was taking no more chances.

As Susan tried frantically to reach her clothes, Cassandra shrieked at the top of her voice, "Oh, no you don't, you little slut. I'll let you out of this door as you are—bare-assed naked. Keep your boa, you piece of trash, but you're not getting your clothes!" As Susan ran past Cassandra as fast as she could, Cassandra roared, "Run, lover-girl, run. You better run before I put a bullet in your skinny ass!" She slammed the door behind the fleeing woman.

All the while, Ravel's *Bolero* continued to play. Fredrick crouched down on the chaise lounge while Cassandra paced the room. They paid no attention to the pulsating rhythm as the muted sounds from the trumpets floated in the air. Fredrick, trying in vain to cover his nakedness, attempted several times to speak with his wife, but she would howl at him and wave her gun his way. Sadie thought that the music would never stop. Cassandra seemed to be in step with the deliberate tapping of the snare drums.

"Cupcake, I thought you were in California," Fredrick finally squeaked out.

"Don't you call me that, you fornicator, you. That's just what I wanted you to think. Dumb ass," Cassandra spit out.

Sadie breathed a sigh of relief when three policemen crashed into the office shouting, "Police. Freeze!" Cassandra dropped the gun on the floor. Fredrick rolled himself into a ball. The police stood there for a bit, taking in the scene. Broken glass and white feathers covered the floor. *Bolero* was still blasting from the stereo. When one policeman pulled the plug, there was dead silence. Then one of them spotted Sadie peeking out the opening in the wall. "Don't move!" he boomed. It didn't take him long before he found Sadie and Mable, with their arms wrapped around each other, trembling, crying, and cowering on the kitchen floor.

"What the hell is going on here?" Police Chief Keller asked. "First, we find a naked woman, wrapped in a feather boa, galloping down the road. Then, we come in here and discover a man wearing another feather boa, sprawled on the sofa. Next, we have a woman brandishing a gun with broken glass all over the floor. Now we have two women, who look like ducks, wearing yellow rubber aprons and gloves. This is either an early Halloween party, or you are all a bit crazy. Call for back up," the Chief ordered, "I'm hauling all their asses in."

Chapter 25

Ellie May couldn't wait until she reached Marty's apartment. She doubted that too many people had heard the latest news, especially since there had been several after-the-prom parties last night. But it was nine and she absolutely couldn't wait another minute to see Marty. She already had called Rosebud and told her to get to Marty's fast.

Just as she was about to ring the doorbell, Rosebud came running down Lilac. "My God, Ellie May, what's so important that we have to meet immediately?"

Ellie May didn't respond. She leaned heavily on Marty's doorbell.

The door opened quickly, "Ellie May, what on earth is wrong?" Marty asked apprehensively.

"*Serenity...Serenity,*" is all Ellie May could get out.

"What about it? What has happened? So help me, Ellie May, stop this fooling around and tell me," Marty ordered.

"She caught them...she caught them. Susan and Fredrick. His wife caught them at *Serenity*," Ellie May responded, trying to catch her breath.

"I *told* you they were messing around, now, didn't I," Rosebud yelped as she placed her hands on her hips.

"You were right, Rosebud. Last night, right after closing, his wife let herself into the restaurant. She went directly to the office, and there, well there, she caught them and I think they were naked! Naked, do you hear? While the reporter didn't actually say that, I believe they were," Ellie May said. "I can't believe they would do such a thing. Apparently his wife had a gun and shot the whole place up."

"No! Was anyone hurt? Marty questioned as she held her hand over her mouth.

"They did say that five people were taken in for questioning. Do you think they were having one of those sex parties?" Ellie May asked timidly.

"Five people? I wonder who they were," Rosebud uttered.

"Just the other night, on *Detective Hour,* they had a story that was close to this whole thing. Well...this woman, a loose woman as they're called, was messing around with a married man and the wife caught on. The wife came up with a unique plan. She went to the mistress' house, pulled her outside, tied her—naked, mind you—tied her to a tree and then went home." Ellie May said dramatically. "Too bad Susan wasn't tied to a tree."

"Ellie May, you really need to change your TV habits a bit," Marty said kiddingly.

'I wonder how his wife set this all up?" Ellie May said.

"What do you mean?" Rosebud asked.

"You don't think she just went to the restaurant on a lark, do you? She planned all this. I'm not sure how, but I bet you she did," Ellie May insisted. "Now what do we do?"

"You mean about Susan and the necklace?" Rosebud asked.

"Sure. How will this affect our investigation?" Ellie May said firmly.

"It's too bad that Susan was having an affair with a married man; I certainly don't condone that. But we have no proof that she has my necklace. She may be a home wrecker, but she really may have no connection to my missing jewelry," Marty reiterated as she began pacing the floor.

"I think we'll have to wait awhile. Hopefully something will happen that may give us new ideas of how to find the necklace," Marty said. "I can go ahead and ask Preston to stop by to give me some ideas on how I can expand the closet in my den, or something similar. That will give me time to get to know him better. But, the more I think about him, I believe we may be chasing a wild goose."

"Marty, I think you should try to meet with him. When I talked with him some time ago, you know that I wasn't successful in getting anything incriminating out of him, but we've got to start again somewhere," Rosebud said.

"Okay, I'll do it. Now, to change the topic. Rosebud, I must tell you how impressed I was last night with the way that you and Nigel took over the dance floor. You were a beautiful Prom Queen. You were fantastic! I knew that you were a good dancer, but I would never have guessed that Nigel could dance like Fred Astaire—he's heavier than Fred, but certainly as light on his feet," Marty said.

"And you, Marty, I saw you and Frank go out the front door last night. Now, young lady, redeem yourself," Rosebud said as she chuckled.

"Frank was a delight. We went out to the gazebo and just talked. We must have been out there for an hour or so," Marty said a little shyly. "I had an enjoyable evening."

"And?" Rosebud said pointedly.

"Well, we'll see. I think we can be good friends. We have much in common," Marty responded.

"Okay, enough about the prom. Now, let's get back to Susan. Where do we go from here?" an impatient Ellie May asked.

"We'll have to wait awhile—till things calm down. I'm certain that it will be all over our local news for days to come. It all depends on Susan," Rosebud said.

"What do you mean 'it depends on Susan'?" Ellie May asked. "She's the one who caused all this, that little trollop."

"Ellie May! I'm surprised at you," Marty chided. "He's as much to blame as she is—in fact more. He's the one who's married. Rosebud meant that we don't know what Susan will do now. She may just leave town."

"If Susan leaves town, it could make it harder for us to get the goods on her," Ellie May said. "The longer it takes to solve a crime, the more difficult it becomes. You know, people die, memories fade…"

"Ellie May, you sound just like a crime show," an exasperated Rosebud said.

"Well, I may watch a lot of crime shows, but I do know that we must be careful what we say to the others about the *Serenity* fiasco. We don't want anyone else to learn about the necklace," Ellie May replied. "As they say on TV, let's play our cards close to our vest."

"I have an idea," Rosebud said. "Let's go to The Square. There's sure to be a gathering there today, especially after the prom. Besides, if others know about what happened at *Serenity,* they will be exchanging the skinny about that, too."

As they walked towards The Square, Ellie May said, "Now remember, look surprised at the news about Fredrick's little love nest gone wrong. Be careful, however, don't add anything to the conversation about why we want to know more about Susan."

Jessie approached Rosebud. "Rosebud, I had no idea that you were such a fabulous dancer. You and Nigel danced as well as any professionals that I have ever seen. And, you looked twenty years younger in that silver gown."

"Thank you, Jessie. Most of the credit for the dancing goes to Nigel. I just followed his lead," Rosebud responded graciously.

"Whoever would have thought that such an annoying person would turn out to be the showpiece of the evening?" Jessie said as she banged her cane on the floor. *"Pretty Rosebud twirled like a top, while her partner looked like a mop."*

While Rosebud giggled, she said, "I thought Nigel was fantastic and he looked great in that tux."

"Yeah, you're right. I just don't like the man, so I apologize to you, Rosebud, but never to Nigel," Jessie said.

"Get ready," Marty whispered to Rosebud, "here comes Abigail."

"Darling," Abigail almost shouted, "you were absolutely fabulous last evening. You and Nigel were amazing. You, in your stunning gown, and Nigel—why he shocked us all."

"Why, thank you, Abigail. You and William certainly made a handsome couple on the dance floor. Isn't it nice that we have some gentlemen here at Morning Glory Hill, who like to dance?" Rosebud said sincerely.

"Talking about my dance partner—here he comes now. Oh, William, good morning. I was expressing my view at how charming she and Nigel were on the dance floor," Abigail said as she slyly placed her hand on William's arm.

"I couldn't agree more," William said. "You two gave all of us inspiration to become better dancers just by your fine example. I would have expected that from you, Rosebud, but we were all surprised at the gracefulness Nigel displayed."

"I also thought the Turnbulls looked fabulous as well has Harry and Harvey. It was so nice seeing so many people dressed so well," Abigail said considerately.

"Did you hear? Did you hear what happened at *Serenity?*" Celeste asked as she joined the group, pulling her book-filled wagon behind her.

"Seems like I've been missing out on what the latest gossip is around here. What about *Serenity?*" Jesse asked.

"Well, it appears that the owner has been fooling around with one of his servers. His wife burst into the restaurant late last night and caught them red-handed—or as gossip has it—bare-assed," Celeste said as she giggled.

While Ellie May appeared to be totally uninterested in the gossip, she was keeping a close watch on her two friends. She knew that they could easily blow their cover if they were not careful.

"I was told that the wife had a gun. Did you hear that?" Celeste asked eagerly.

"No, I didn't hear that," Ellie May responded.

When Rosebud spotted Nigel heading towards the group, she said quickly, "Oh, here comes my luncheon date. I'll see you later," she said as she hurried to meet Nigel.

The senior citizens, who had been exchanging theories about the wife's method of discovery about her philandering husband, now looked a little strange, standing there with their mouths wide opened, as they watched the two hurry down the hall to *The Sassy Cat.*

Jesse smiled. "Well, I'll be. Dancing's one thing, having lunch is *quite* another."

Celeste took hold of the handle of her wagon and said, "You just never know—you just never know. Who said that life in a senior retirement campus was boring? I've got some new books in the wagon—anyone interested? Or do you find it juicer just to watch the residents?"

Jessie didn't hear what Celeste had just said—she was more interested in Rosebud and Nigel. "That is too bizarre even for me to make up a rhyme!"

Chapter 26

Samuel Long had his arms full as he opened his apartment door. He stepped inside and kicked the door closed with his foot. Oscar, his Siamese cat, was curled up on the middle cushion of the sofa. "Oh, you lazy fellow," Samuel said, "you can't even get up to greet the person who feeds you every day." Samuel put his groceries on the kitchen table and began to put things away. Oscar barely lifted his head to see what was going on. But, it was Oscar's attitude and his ability to ignore people that made Samuel love him so much. The two of them were quite alike. Oscar had almond-shaped blue eyes that made his silver coat shine even brighter. He seemed to enjoy showing off his muscular body—a trait that his owner also had.

Oscar particularly didn't like females. The few times that women had been in the apartment, Samuel had had to keep Oscar at bay. The cat had the habit of strutting back and forth in front of a woman, all the while glaring and mewing at her just to let her know that she displeased him. Samuel had to admit that he felt almost the same way about women. Long ago, when Samuel had tried to connect with women, it had always failed. Eventually, he had given up and adopted the life of a confirmed bachelor.

Samuel sat down on the sofa next to Oscar. "Well, Oscar, old boy. I have to tell you that I thought that stupid prom was a bore. I only went to take pictures and to pick up some tidbits for my book. You should have seen them, Oscar. The men made complete asses of themselves, dancing around like chickens—mind you, like chickens! But I did spot some interesting *pairings* —you know—like William and Abigail, and now, apparently Marty and Frank. I'm surprised at Frank. I thought he knew better than to get mixed up with a female this late in his life. However, I wasn't surprised at William—he's always flirting. But Frank—well, I was shocked. That man is worth a lot of money and I bet you anything that that opportunist Marty knows that and has set her cap for him. The darned old fool."

Once again, Samuel began searching the Internet, looking for anything about anyone that he could use for his book. He decided that he would look into that little jockey fellow, Stretch, the so-called baker, to find out why he's now a baker. Heaven only knows what terrible things had happened at the race track. "Let's see, Oscar. I'll put his name in, *Andrew Cutler*, and see what I can find. Maybe he's connected to someone who lives here. You know, Oscar, if people were more like cats, they would be smarter. People trust other people too much. Bingo! Look here, Oscar, I found something." Oscar, stared at Samuel for a disinterested minute, then laid his head back down on the cushion.

Samuel was lost in his search. "Listen to this. Andrew had ridden a horse named MONKEY *BUSINESS* in a stakes race and the horse was later disqualified for doping. Of course, Andrew had claimed that he knew nothing about the horse being given drugs and swore that he had never been around the horse other than to ride him in a race. See Oscar, all one has to do is to look hard enough, long enough, and in as many web sites as possible, and one can find out all kinds of things."

Samuel read several articles about the scandal, but he didn't find any connection to anyone at Morning Glory Hill. Meanwhile, Oscar gracefully jumped off the sofa and strutted around the living room. Samuel shifted gears. Next, he chose one of the women. He would see what he could find about *her*. He became occupied in searching and was finally rewarded. This could really be an explosive part of his book. He spent over an hour, searching and making copious notes. Who would have guessed it? He was certain that he was probably the only one who knew anything about her sordid past. He could stretch this incident out into a whole chapter. What luck!

He was taking great care with each sentence he wrote. While he could not call his characters by their true names, they would know that he was talking about them. How delicious! The idea of getting his revenge on those he disliked so much excited him. It will be fun to watch them squirm like worms on a hotplate.

He turned the TV on. By now, more facts about the juicy event that happened at *Serenity* should be on the late news.

"Well, Oscar, this may help me make my book more salacious. Where there is one fornicator, there may be another."

Oscar jumped back up and lay in Samuel's lap. "Oh, good boy." Samuel said. "You are my buddy, aren't you? We are so alike. What do you think, Oscar? With what I found out about our little baker man and the past history of one of our fine *ladies*, I'll have great fodder for my manuscript. Now, if I can connect *Serenity* to all of this, I may have to turn it into a trilogy. I'll change their names and their appearances. Oh, this is going to be so amusing." When Samuel stood up, Oscar slid unceremoniously onto the floor. "Sorry, Oscar, I need to get to The Square. With everything that happened last night, I need to get the latest. Looks like my book may be writing itself."

Chapter 27

Marty decided that it was time to meet with Preston. If they were ever going to find out if he had anything to do with her missing necklace, she needed to get to work. She went over several scenarios in her mind regarding her reason for the meeting. It could be that she wanted her closet extended, or maybe she could get her living room walls painted. Celeste had had her walls painted and Marty was very impressed at how it seemed to elevate the beauty of the room. She had hoped that Rosebud's friend—the one who had discovered that Susan had paid cash for a new car—could do some leg work, but, unfortunately, he had taken a government job that prohibited him from doing any outside detective work. Picking up the phone, she dialed Mary Beth and made an appointment with Preston to discuss painting the living room.

As she hung up the phone, the doorbell rang. She was surprised to see Frank. "Why, Frank, how nice to see you again."

"My daughter dropped off copies of the photos she took of us. She even put one in a little frame. I hope you like them," Frank said as he hung back a bit.

"Come in, come in, Frank. Oh, these are so nice. And, this one in the frame is absolutely wonderful. It was so sweet of her to do this, Frank. Please let me have her address so that I can send her a thank you card."

Frank took a seat on the sofa. As he shuffled his feet around, he also began playing with his watch. Taking a breath, he said, "Marty, I want to thank you again for going to the prom with me. It was such a nice evening." As he spotted some color charts on the end table, he asked, "Are you planning on getting some painting done?" He tried to hide his trembling hands.

"I haven't made up my mind for sure, yet, but I think I'd like to paint my living room walls. I really hate the look of all white. It seems to

take away from the beauty of the furniture. What do you think, Frank?"
"I'm not such a good decorator. I have a difficult time telling one shade
from another," Frank replied. Taking a few gulps, he said, "I am also
here to invite you to a cookout next Sunday. My daughters are having
a family gathering and they would like you to join us." He could feel
the sweat rolling down his back.

"That sounds like fun, Frank. I'd really like that."

"Delores said she would pick us up around noon. Will that be okay
with you?" Frank said hopefully. Frank stood up. "I'd best be going
now. Oh, first, I'll write my daughter's address down for you...you
know, for the thank you card you mentioned."

Marty closed the door gently behind Frank. She had liked Frank
from the moment that she had met him, but now—well, now, she had
a different feeling about him. She sat down on the sofa and picked up
the framed picture Frank had just brought her. She was surprised at
how nice they looked together. A feeling came over her—one that
she hadn't felt in a long time. Could it be that the two of them were
merely developing a friendship, or was it possible that it was evolving
into a relationship—one heard so much about *relationships* nowadays.
In fact, two of her grandchildren claimed that they were in one rather
than a marriage. Well, if youngsters could do that, why not seniors?
Marty considered this for a moment and then thought: comfortable
and content—*that* was it. *That's how she feels whenever she is around Frank.*

Chapter 28

"But, Harvey, if we get involved in something like that, we would be right back in the same situation that we were in before we moved to Morning Glory Hill," a frustrated Harry said. "We were both tired of the rat race life we were living, and we wanted peace and quiet with lots of time to travel."

"I know, I know, but owning a shop like *Marie's Closet* would be such fun," Harvey argued.

"Fun? Don't forget about all the hours that we would have to put in just to make a profit. We really don't need to do that, Harvey. With our investments, we're doing just fine. Look, Marie's husband is anxious for her to get out of business because it eats up so much of her time," Harry said as he slumped down in his favorite chair. "Are you finding being home with me boring?"

"Now that's not fair," Harvey said intensely as he pursed his lips. "Our marriage is fine and you know that I love you. I guess I got carried away at the thought of getting back into business again."

It was quiet for several minutes. Then Harvey jumped up and said, "Let's consider the subject closed," he encouraged. "C'mon. Let's take a walk. It's such a gorgeous day. Take your camera along in case you're inspired with anything you see along the way. You have those contests coming up in a few months, so let's go looking for subjects. We'll go through The Square. That way we can pick up our mail."

As Harvey was pulling out the mail from their box, Rosebud came up behind them and said, "Hi, guys. How are you two today?"

"We're fine, Rosebud. Have you recuperated from all that dancing the other night?" Harry teased.

"Wasn't that fun? We need to plan more nights like that," Rosebud suggested.

"You and Nigel were a delight to watch," Harvey said.

"Well, we had to work hard to keep up with you two," Rosebud ribbed.

"Is this a mutual admiration club?" Ellie May said as she joined the group.

"We're headed out for a picture-taking session," Harvey said. "You know, Harry is quite an excellent photographer. In fact, he's had several of his photos published in magazines. Stop by our place any time and I'll show you some of his best work."

As Harry and Harvey walked away, Ellie May said, "Those two never cease to amaze me. They're so talented. Oh, that's my cell phone."

Rosebud turned away to give her friend privacy. Suddenly, Ellie May tapped her on the shoulder and said, "Marty needs us right away." Then, in a whisper, she said, "It's about the necklace."

As they neared Marty's apartment, they saw that she was waiting for them at the door. They hurried inside. "Marty, you look pale. What's happened?" Rosebud asked.

"It could even be worse than I had imagined," Marty said, obviously upset.

"What? What?" Ellie May said as she took Marty's hand to comfort her.

"Let me tell you this from the beginning. When my husband was growing up, he lived alongside a family named Martindale. My husband and the youngest Martindale boy, Randy, became close friends. In fact, Randy was the best man at our wedding. They kind of lost touch with one another over the years; but every now and then, they would have an opportunity to spend some time together," Marty said. "Forgive me if I ramble. I need to get all this out before I lose my mind. Well, anyway, Randy's wife, Victoria, dropped by to see me this morning to give me a birthday present. I'm not sure why she remembered my birthday after all these years."

Marty grew quiet for a few seconds to gather her thoughts. "I thought it strange because I haven't seen her in many years. But, when she said that she was in the area to collect insurance on a claim that she had filed on a missing diamond necklace, she really shook me up. She went on to tell me the investigation took three years and she had begun to think that she would never get paid."

"Wow, Marty, how did you keep your cool?" a concerned Rosebud asked.

"No wonder you're upset," Ellie May said in a comforting tone. "What do you make of all this now?"

"I think there are two possible scenarios. One is that the necklace I had was the real one. If so, it might mean that my husband had taken part in an insurance scam. The other is that the thief got the real one and the necklace that I had was the fake one. However, if either one is true, that means my Charlie had dirty hands." Marty paused. "I believe Victoria wanted me to know about the necklace. I think she was looking for one or both! She used the ploy of remembering my birthday to find out if I knew anything about the necklace. She was digging, hoping to hit pay dirt. She even mentioned that a paste replica of the necklace was also stolen."

"In other words, Victoria was on a fishing expedition. She was definitely looking for information. Did you say anything about your necklace," Ellie May quizzed.

"No. I didn't trust her. I suspected her motives almost immediately. Suppose their whole family was in on the scam? Look, is it possible that they still have the real one hidden somewhere and now they want to get the fake one back, too?" Marty put her head down. Heaving a sigh, she said, "I'm beginning to hate that damned necklace." The sobs grew louder.

"Marty, don't cry. We're going to help you sort this out. If Charlie was part of an insurance scam, you had nothing to do with that. But we really don't know that he did anything wrong," Ellie May said reassuringly. "Let's not paint him with a broad brush at this point in time."

Rosebud said, "Remember, Charlie may not have done anything illegal. To bring you peace of mind, we need to find your necklace. Then, whether it is real or not, you can make an informed decision about how you want to proceed. But, Marty, remember: even if he had been involved somehow in this fiasco, you don't know why. He may have had a good reason. Keep the faith, Marty. Ellie May and I are here for you."

Chapter 29

Preston was laying down tarps when Marty came into the living room. "Is there anything that I can do to help you?" she asked the maintenance man.

"No, Mrs. Miller. I think I have everything I need," Preston replied.

"Do you mind if I watch you for a while?" Marty said as she pulled a chair up on the other side of the room. "I'm anxious to see the color."

"That's fine with me. It does get kinda lonely when you have several walls to paint. By the way, you chose a very nice complimentary color," Preston said as he got his long-handled roller ready.

Marty was quiet for a few minutes. She wanted to ask him lots of questions, but she wasn't sure how to begin. "Do you live nearby?"

"Sure do. We just moved to Meadow Lark Road. My wife and I, and our two sons, really like the area," Preston said, as he put the first color on the wall.

"How old are your sons?"

"My youngest is fifteen and my oldest boy just graduated from high school. And, I'm proud to say that he'll be attending Temple University in September. I don't think my other son wants to go to college—all he talks about is music. He's formed a little band and, my oh my, when they practice, I have to put cotton in my ears," Preston said as he laughed.

"Well, you never know. He may make it big. Some of the groups I hear on TV sound more like cats crying," Marty replied. "I don't always understand the songs they sing, but I guess that's just because I've been out of the loop for some time now," Marty said as she chuckled. "But, then again, I can remember when my mom said the same thing when I would play my records and jitterbug all over the living room."

"Yeah, I know what you mean. I really want him to go to college, too, just in case the music thing doesn't work out. But it'll be his decision," Preston said as he moved the ladder a few feet.

Marty watched in silence for a few minutes. She jumped when the doorbell rang. "Come in," Marty called.

"Oh, sorry, Marty, I forgot you're having some painting done today. I was just going to invite you to lunch," Rosebud said apologetically.

"Preston, I'll be in *The Sassy Cat Café* in case you need me for anything," Marty said. She saw that Rosebud was looking at her peculiarly, so she gave her a reassuring smile.

"Have a nice lunch, ladies," Preston said.

As they proceeded down the hallway to the cafe, Marty said, "Look, Rosebud, I have to trust the man. As far as I know, he's innocent. He's a family man."

"Oh, family men are all honest?" Rosebud questioned.

"My bedroom door is locked, so my valuables are safe. I just can't go through my life not trusting people. I did discover two interesting things about him, though: he just moved his family to Meadow Lark Road and his son will be entering Temple this fall."

"My goodness, Marty, you are some kind of detective. Ellie May will be proud of you," Rosebud said happily. "Did you also find out if he goes to the dentist regularly?"

"What? Dentist?" Marty asked dumbfounded.

"Just a little joke. It's the kind Nigel pulls all the time," Rosebud said.

"Wait just a minute. Now you're sounding like Nigel," Marty teased.

"Well, Nigel can be funny at times. He's really a teddy bear underneath that slightly rotund body," Rosebud said as she giggled. Eager to get the conversation away from Nigel, she said, "Have you heard from Frank lately?"

"Funny you should ask—yes. I've been invited to a family cookout tomorrow," Marty said joyfully.

"My God, he's introducing you to his family already! Marty, you're a fast worker."

"Rosebud, it's just a family gathering. Don't make too much out of it," Marty encouraged. "Now, how can we check into Preston's new home and his son's acceptance at Temple? These things all cost money."

Chapter 30

Harvey, with clipboard in hand, was handing out tickets to those people going to the ballgame. "Now, hang on to these, folks. We have great seats, and luckily, they're under the overhang so you'll be in the shade. I encourage you to wear your sunglasses anyway since the sun will be very bright. By the way, there are going to be lots of prizes given away today so keep your numbered stubs."

The group of twenty going to the afternoon ballgame was seated in The Square waiting for the bus. Harry had his camera equipment on his lap and was tapping his one foot on the floor—eager to get underway. He hated waiting for almost anything. While baseball could not be counted as one of his favorite activities, he thought he just might find some interesting things to capture with his camera. And, since Harvey loved baseball, Harry was willing to tolerate at least one more game.

William, who was holding Abigail's straw hat while she was getting her sunglasses out of her matching bag, was aglow. He thought of himself as a new man—a sort of born-again man—since he had met Abigail. "Great day for a ballgame," William said to Harvey.

"Any day is good for baseball," Harvey said with a smile.

Abigail spotted Gordon and Marie making their way across The Square. "Marie," she called, and quickly moved over to make room for her friend on the couch. During the past few weeks, the two couples had gone out for dinner several times and had even attended a local festival together. Marie knew very little about baseball and Abigail had promised to explain things to her as they occurred on the field.

"Hey, hey, I'm here, folks," Nigel said as he appeared with Rosebud. "Now the fun will begin."

Stretch came running across The Square. "I thought you might leave without me. I wasn't sure that Hortense would approve of my going along with the residents, but she finally did." He handed Harvey a bag and said, "Here, I made these cookies at home. I thought they might be good to munch on. What do you think?"

"Thanks, Stretch. Even if our team loses, we'll enjoy your treat. Now, folks, I want to share some information with you, so listen carefully. We have twenty great seats. Make sure you stay together as we enter the ball park. I believe the game is sold out today. There's a great deli on the third floor deck that serves everything from pizza to French fries," Harvey explained. "I have paper fans for the ladies."

"Oh, just for the ladies?" Nigel questioned.

"I heard you were a ladies' man, Nigel," Harvey teased. "I would think you would be in favor of taking care of them."

"I always treat ladies with care," Nigel responded. "Why, on our twenty-fifth anniversary, I treated my wife to a trip to China!"

"That was nice, Nigel," Harvey said.

"And, on our fiftieth, I'll go back and pick her up," Nigel replied.

Rosebud giggled. "Nigel, you are a naughty boy. You're such a tease."

Abigail wanted desperately to ask Nigel not to be so juvenile, but she held her tongue. She looked over at William, and she suddenly felt blessed. As long as William was by her side, she could tolerate that obnoxious Nigel.

"The bus is here. Ladies and gentlemen, I hope you enjoy your day," Harvey said as he escorted his group outside.

As the group proceeded in an orderly fashion, Sally took off running and was successful in getting on the bus first. With a self-satisfied look on her face, she settled into the first seat.

Marty arrived just in time to wave goodbye to Rosebud. She was surprised to see Preston standing by the front door talking with a lady.

"You're not going to the ballgame?" Hortense asked Marty.

"Not this time," Marty responded. "Hortense, who was the lady talking with Preston?"

"That's Beryl, his wife. She's such a prudent person. For the first two years of their marriage, she worked and saved every penny for the education of their kids. She was determined that she was not going to have children until their college money was tucked away in the bank."

Chapter 31

"Now that we know how Preston was able to send his son to college, we can cross one thing off our investigation list," Ellie May said. "But, how do we find out about the money Preston used to purchase a new home?"

"For heaven's sake," Rosebud said, he worked in construction for years. I'm certain that he wasn't at the bottom of the salary scale. And, if his wife was so good at handling money to get their children in college, I'm certain that she was thrifty. I think we need to get back to tracking Susan."

Marty was seated between her friends in the gazebo. It was a mild, early September day. Thoughts of her Charlie ever being involved in fraud often made her quite sick in her stomach. "I believe that Preston had nothing to do with my necklace. I wish I could stop thinking of it as *my* necklace. But I truly would like to straighten this mess out once and for all. It seems to bring a cloud of suspicion over everything and I don't like that at all."

"Is there a way you could befriend his wife?" Ellie May asked.

"I couldn't do that. Befriend her in order to incriminate her husband? You have to be joking," Marty said harshly.

"I apologize for that," Ellie May said. "I really didn't want to offend you, Marty."

"I know you didn't." Marty responded. "I've even thought about hiring a detective to find out more about Susan. She's a much more viable candidate to be classified as a thief. After all, she tried stealing a husband, but that didn't work out very well, did it?"

"You can say that again," Rosebud said.

"I haven't shared any of this with my son. If his dad was involved, I didn't want Daniel to know. Also, he would be hurt that I didn't tell him about the necklace right away. But he adored Charlie, and I don't want that to change. Geez, look what I've created," Marty said.

"Marty, don't give up now. The three of us can come up with something—I'm certain of that," Ellie May said assuredly. "Let's ride this out for a while and see which way the wind blows. Very often, when a crime goes cold, something occurs which clarifies everything. I recommend we take a break from this, have some fun, get involved in other things, and if and when some solid evidence pops up, then we'll resume our investigation."

"We can volunteer to be hostesses for the children's concert. That will be held in three weeks and should be a lot of fun," Marty suggested.

"We might be having a wedding here before too long," Rosebud said, as she arched her eyebrows.

Ellie May looked at her friend in amazement, "No—you and Nigel?"

"Goodness, no, Ellie May. I mean this thing with William and Abigail is really getting heavy. Don't you think?" Rosebud asked.

"Well," Ellie May said as she placed her hand on her chin, "I think they owe us a reward. After all, we set the whole thing up through *Operation Smile!*"

"Maybe they would have found each other anyway," Rosebud said.

They each appeared to be lost in their thoughts for a while. Finally, Ellie May said, as she leaned in closer to her friends, "I did think of one other possibility about the necklace." "Perhaps the person who took your necklace was really a *bagman*."

"Here comes one of your *True Crime* stories," Rosebud cautioned.

"A *bagman* is a person who carries something, usually something illegal, from one place to another in order to earn cash. Maybe Susan was one of these. She had access to something someone wanted—your necklace. She would then take it and give it to the person who hired her. She has the morals of a snake, so it's possible."

"But who would know where the necklace was?" Rosebud asked.

"The person who gave it to Charlie," Ellie May said convincingly.

Marty sat up straight. "Ellie May, you may have hit on something here. If someone in the Martindale family gave it to Charlie, that person would definitely know where it was. Maybe that's the real reason Victoria came to see me She was hoping that I would tell her something about the necklace. I thought it strange that she would remember my birthday after all this time. If she was looking for information, it means that my necklace did not make it back to the Martindale family."

"So where is the necklace now?" Rosebud asked. "The more we get involved in this mystery, the more certain I am that you had the real necklace. We just can't sit on this. We must move forward before the trail gets cold."

"Now who's sounding like *CSI?*" Ellie May asked.

Chapter 32

Abigail was seated at her vanity table, absently brushing her hair. She was looking forward to the concert her little ones from the elementary school would be putting on today in the dining room. Every time she thought about the children, she smiled. When she had first moved into Morning Glory Hill, she had been an angry, despondent woman—one who saw joy in nothing. Then, through a chance meeting with an old friend, she discovered the school was looking for volunteers for various events and, for some reason, her heart and her mind seized the opportunity to get out and do something with her life.

For many years, Abigail had been an unhappy, neglected wife of a bank president. She had dreamed of having children. When she didn't become pregnant, her husband had blamed her. Her pleas that he should visit his doctor had gone unheeded for many years. When he finally had given in and made an appointment, it was the beginning of a *cat and mouse* situation between the two of them. When he had realized that he could never impregnate a woman, he began having one affair after another, never bothering to hide these trysts from her. Their marriage had deteriorated and their lives took separate paths. She became lonely, bitter and disenfranchised. Her only solace—her only link to sanity—were the times when she sang—either paid performances, or those she did for various charities.

While she had considered leaving him many times, she stayed. She would stay for the money—a substantial amount. He had invested both his money and Abigail's in Apple Computers. When he died of a massive heart attack, Abigail performed all the duties of a devoted wife, and then she sat back while the checks rolled in. She looked at herself in the mirror and wondered if she would burn in Hell for the relief she felt when he finally breathed his last breath.

When a friend discovered that there were children from poor families, who wanted to learn to play an instrument that their families could not afford, she sprang into action. She had no one to pass her fortune on to anyway, so why not share the money with these delightful children. Remarkably, this little group of fledgling musicians had given her a lifeline to happiness.

When she had moved into Morning Glory Hill, she was certain that all the residents knew about her philandering husband—she could see it in their eyes—judging her—making fun of her. But the longer she worked with the children, the softer she had become. And, now, there was William. She could lower that protective shield that she had carried for so long. She liked the feeling of generosity. Yes, it was a gamble, but it felt so good—so right.

Abigail was taking her time choosing an outfit to wear to the concert. Not only did she want to please the children, she also wanted to look her best for William. She had been drawn to him in a haunting way. He was on her mind constantly. However, his reputation as a womanizer had worried her at first—she had been there—done that—and she would not do *that* again. She could not deny it—there was definitely a mystique about the piano player. Her dearest friend used to tell her that *love comes dressed in many packages.* She never understood that little saying until now.

As she entered the dining room, Barry and Harvey were placing name cards on the tables. Five orchestra members would be seated at each table where they would be hosted by three residents. Each table had little replicas of various instruments scattered across the table top. A centerpiece of a miniature gold tuba, with musical notes spewing out of its bell, created an appropriate atmosphere for the concert. At each child's place was a little silver gift bag, filled with small delights that Abigail had provided.

"Gentlemen," Abigail said cheerfully, "how wonderful this place looks. My little musicians will really love it."

"Do your workers get a grab bag, too, Abigail?" Harvey teased. "You are spoiling these kids."

"That's what adopted grandmothers are for," Abigail said, obviously pleased with the room arrangement. "I see that you have the stage set up, too."

"We must confess. The director was here very early this morning to give us the plans for that," Barry said.

Meanwhile, the school buses pulled up to the front door of Morning Glory Hill. Hortense was waiting outside to greet the children and to give directions to the adults who would be taking the instruments and other orchestra paraphernalia to the back door. She was pleased that the chaperones were taking good care of the children. The girls were wearing white blouses, black pleated skirts and black shoes, while the boys looked so professional with their white shirts, black bow ties, black trousers and shoes.

As the youngsters filed through the doors, the residents seated in The Square, applauded. The children smiled and waved. Sally stood up and hurried to the dining room.

"Aren't they just adorable?" Jessie remarked. *"Black and white, black and white, oh, how nice, oh how bright."*

"That's not one of your best ones, Jessie," Nigel teased.

As the children entered the dining room, Abigail was there to meet them. When they spotted her, they rushed to her side. "Miss Abigail, Miss Abigail, I want to have lunch with you," one child said.

"Well, the people who live here just can't wait to have lunch with all of you. So, to be fair to my neighbors, you'll be seated with them. To brighten your day even further, you'll find a little bag at your place with a few goodies just for you."

When the children heard this, they jumped up and down. "Miss Abigail, you are the bestest person I ever did know," a little boy said, obviously enthralled with Abigail. "Sorry, Miss Abigail, I mean the best. I know there is no such word as *bestest*."

"My, my, Corey. You not only play the violin very well, you are speaking better each day," she said as she patted him on his back.

It didn't take long to get the children seated. The smiles on the faces of the adults as the children introduced themselves to their hosts warmed Abigail's heart. She was thrilled that they loved them as much as she did. Abigail flitted from table to table, making sure that all was well. When the wait staff arrived with large trays of pizza pie, the children cheered.

"Now, don't forget to eat your fruit," Abigail said as she walked among the tables. "Musicians need strong, healthy bodies to be able to play their instruments."

Abigail owned this moment—among the children who loved her. More importantly, she fully understood that they gave her more than she would ever be able to repay.

The chaperones were finally able to get the children ready to mount the stage and take their places to begin the concert. When they were quiet, their director, Mr. Hoch, moved to the microphone. "The children and I wish to thank you for your warm invitation to come here to entertain you. We have chosen a few songs that we think you may enjoy. The children have worked diligently to prepare for this little concert. So, sit back, relax, and listen to the music."

When the first notes of *Serenade for Strings* floated through the air, the audience was all smiles. After the last notes were played, the audience responded with applause. Mr. Hoch motioned for his string section to stand. Selections from *The Sleeping Beauty and The Seven Dwarfs* were next.

The next piece was an updated version of *Twinkle, Twinkle Little Star*. As they played, little silver stars fell from the dining room ceiling. The audience was so enthralled that they gave the children a standing ovation. Harvey was standing behind the curtain and was relieved that the contraption that he had rigged in the ceiling had worked flawlessly.

When they played *God Bless America,* the audience stood once again. After the applause died down, Mr. Hoch picked up the mike again. "The children have a special presentation to make to Miss Abigail," he said. "Miss Abigail, will you please join us on the stage?"

Abigail was genuinely surprised as she approached the stage. Her eyes welled up. Two children approached the center of the stage, carrying bouquets of flowers in their arms.

"Miss Abigail," the boy began, "you are our angel. You have taken us under your wings, allowing us to become musicians."

"Miss Abigail," the girl said, "you not only helped us to create an orchestra, you are always so kind and loving, even when we hit a wrong note."

The audience laughed softly. Abigail took a deep breath and said, "Children, it is I who owe you a debt of gratitude. You replaced depression with joy, you chased the rain and brought me a rainbow, but most of all, you gave me love. Thank you, my precious ones."

William, who was sitting in the rear of the room, had never felt such a sense of affection. No wonder he had fallen in love with this woman. After all the others, he had finally found *the one.*

Chapter 33

The Square in Morning Glory Hill was alive with activity. It was a perfect day for the western barbeque. Frank and Marty were standing with a group chatting about everyday things when Ellie May came rushing toward them.

"Marty, wait till you hear what I just learned. You won't believe this—you just won't believe it," Ellie May said as she tried to catch her breath.

Marty turned to her friend immediately, and, with concern in her voice, she said, "Ellie May, are you alright?"

"Yes, yes, but I have news for all of you," she said with a smile on her face.

Rosebud, Nigel and Celeste formed a tighter circle, leaning in closer to Ellie May.

"A friend of mine stopped by to pick up some items that I'm donating to their yard sale and she almost knocked me over! I finally got the whole story about what happened at *Serenity*. Anyway, her cousin used to work as a cleaning lady for the restaurant and she saw the whole thing," Ellie May said with a sly look on her face.

"You don't mean that episode involving Susan, do you?" Marty asked.

"What other thing happened there?" Ellie May asked incredulously. "Of course, that's what I mean. It seems that her cousin and another cleaning lady were the witnesses. She said that Susan and the owner were naked and dancing all around his office with long feather boas wrapped around themselves."

"Oh, good grief," Rosebud said. "That had to be a funny sight."

Elli May sighed. She was annoyed that she had been interrupted with her story. "Well, as I was saying, all of a sudden the owner's wife pops in the door, waving a gun around. Her cousin almost fainted when the gun went off."

"Oh, did she hit anyone?" a concerned Marty asked.

"Nah. Her cousin said the husband and his mistress were on the other side of the room. But she did hit a prized photograph of Cheney that was hanging on the wall and then she chased Susan out of the office without any clothes on. Then the cops came and took them all to the precinct. Her cousin and her friend were released, but the owner's wife was held and is out on bail. My friend thinks the wife should be charged with attempted murder!" Ellie May said excitedly.

"Maybe, but I don't think so," Frank said. "If the two witnesses testify that she didn't aim at anyone, she just may have to face aggravated assault."

"I think it's hilarious that she aimed at the picture of Cheney. She had to be a Democrat." Nigel added as he laughed.

"I would have paid to see that," Rosebud said. "It had to be like the *Keystone Kops*!"

"Who is Susan?" Celeste asked.

Ellie May quickly said, "She was a server at the restaurant."

"She served the boss very well," Nigel teased as he shook his head in agreement.

Their conversation was interrupted when they heard the sound of an old-fashioned dinner bell ringing. As they moved down the hallway, Sally rushed by them.

"See that? She never changes. Whenever we have to lineup for something, she's always the first in line. Someday, I'm gonna grab her and make her go to the back. She really pisses me off," Nigel said angrily. "To make matters worse, she always chews with her mouth open."

"Now, Nigel, don't get upset," Rosebud coaxed.

"Well, maybe that's why she's so fat," Nigel said. "But I guess I don't have room in that department to talk," Nigel said as he sulked.

"Oh, listen, that must be William playing," Rosebud chirped.

As the residents moved through the buffet, many of them were singing along with William as he played. The aroma of the cooked meat filled the air and laughter could be heard everywhere. It was obvious that they were having a good time.

"Look," Nigel said as he tapped Rosebud's arm, "There she goes—Fatty Arbuckle is once again the first one served."

After everyone had been through the line, William pulled a small microphone from under his piano and said, "Folks, as you probably noticed, I love Garth Brooks. I'm going to sing along with a few of them."

When he finished *The Thunder Rolls*, the crowd applauded loudly. "I have a special one to play for all my friends." As soon as he began playing *Friends in Low Places*, the crowd hooted and hollered. "Now, my final song is for all you romantics." As the strains of *If Tomorrow Never Comes* floated through the air, William looked directly at Abigail. When he sang, *if I never wake up in the morning/will she know how much I love her?*, it was as if there were only two people in the room. Abigail returned his smile, sharing a precious moment.

Later that night, phones were ringing off the hook with the latest skinny about *Serenity* as well as the looks exchanged between William and Abigail.

Chapter 34

Samuel was once again preparing for the Mayors Council meeting. Since there had been so many activities during the past month, he wasn't certain that the Council members would like his idea for another one. After all, from time to time, they would complain to him about how tired they were. Samuel couldn't understand that. He was as old as most of them and his energy level was still high—maybe not as high as it had been, but certainly better than most of the residents. He chalked this off to their lack of doing things to generate or strengthen their brain cells. Samuel lived by the philosophy that one must never stop learning. While he never mentioned to anyone that he held a doctorate, he felt that most of them stopped learning a long time ago. Well, then again, there were those who got interested in computers, iPads, and such. He would give them credit for that.

Serving as a host for the orchestra the other day was something he had surprisingly enjoyed. He could sense the eagerness of the children to learn new things. Perhaps he should follow Abigail's lead and volunteer at the school, or maybe he could start a local history club. The more he thought about this, the more he liked the idea. Maybe he could meet with Abigail after the meeting and get her reaction.

As the members of the Council filed in, Samuel handed out agendas and greeted each one warmly. This was a bit unusual for him since he usually kept some distance between himself and the participants. However, his contentment was rattled when he spotted Harvey entering the room. He simply did not like that man. Whenever there was an event of any kind, the ubiquitous Harvey always seemed to be right in the middle. Samuel felt that perhaps he might accept Harvey—at least in time—but right now the man just annoyed the hell out of him.

Once the meeting got started, Samuel was able to regain his composure and carry on his duties as president. "Well, I am pleased that so many of you enjoyed the concert. Abigail, the children obviously love you and appreciate your efforts." He paused as the members applauded. "I have had a call from the group that runs charity events for the *Children's Hospital of Springdale*. They would like to run a casino night in our dining room as well as the extended space beyond. Hortense has already given her permission contingent upon the approval of the residents. As you know, the extended space is available for clubs and such to hold conferences and special events. The club will supply all the gaming equipment as well as the people to operate the tables and deal cards and provide prizes for the auction."

"Oh, this sounds like fun," Jessie said.

"Samuel, I assume the public will be invited. How will this be handled?" Abigail asked.

"First of all, the charity plans on limiting the sale of tickets to three hundred people. Tickets will be one hundred dollars per person. Everyone will receive a bag of chips..."

"Chips? Why do they need potato chips?" Jessie asked.

"Not potato chips, Jessie, gambling chips. Anyway, for each bag of chips purchased, the buyer will receive $500 worth of chips and one ticket for the big drawing. Buyers can then use those chips to play any of the games they like. And, after two hours of gaming, they will cash in all their remaining chips for play money. Then, there will be an auction. Using their play money, participants will be able to bid on a variety of prizes that will be donated. There will be gift certificates from merchants and restaurants, appliances, jewelry, and other valuable prizes," Samuel explained. "In addition, every time a person buys a bag of chips, they will receive a ticket for the big drawing."

"And what is the prize for the big drawing?" Nigel asked.

"Wait till you hear this," Samuel said, obviously pleased with what he was about to reveal. "Three people will win an all -expenses paid vacation. One will be a ten-day cruise to the Caribbean; the next is a trip to Las Vegas, along with one thousand dollars in cash; and the third one is a one-week trip, flying first-class to Hawaii. What about that?" Samuel said proudly. "Keep in mind, folks, this is for charity."

"What if I don't have any chips left at the end of the gaming?" Nigel asked.

"You will still have one ticket for the big drawing. If you would like to purchase another ticket for the drawing, then that will cost you another hundred bucks," Samuel said.

Celeste raised her hand. "Samuel, I'm concerned about one thing. There are some residents that are opposed to gambling. How would we handle their objections?"

"That's a good point," Marty added. "While I'm all for supporting the hospital, we must not offend anyone."

"I find one problem with this," Ellie May said. "Since the public will be invited, we must make certain that access to our lanes is limited to residents only—security for us is vital."

"That's an excellent point, too. We can make certain that safety is maintained. I'll make certain of that." Samuel offered.

"May I add something to this conversation?" Barry asked.

"Certainly."

"There are no rules or regulations regarding gambling as far as your independent living contracts are concerned. While some may be opposed to gambling, they are not required to attend this function," Barry stated. "However, I think we need to make certain that if there *are* objections, those people be heard. Hortense can handle that situation."

After putting the idea up for a vote, it was obvious that there were no objections from the Council. Samuel had never followed *Roberts' Rules of Order*—he viewed them as old-fashioned, pointless, and time-consuming. After all, he couldn't think of anything that he couldn't handle as long as he got his own way.

"Abigail, would you mind staying a few minutes. I have something that I'd like to discuss with you," Samuel said as the room began to empty out.

As William walked out of the room, he glared at Samuel. While he was willing to wait outside for Abigail, he left the door wide open. If that old geezer made one move on his woman, William would teach him a lesson.

No one seemed to notice William's concern except Celeste. She walked over to William, leaned close to his ear, and said, "I don't blame you, William, I never did trust that Samuel. I may be wrong, but that man is up to something. I can't put my finger on it, but I just sense that he should not be trusted with *anything*."

Chapter 35

Marty was on her way to the dining room to meet Frank for dinner. She thought that it was perhaps time to invite him to her place for a home-cooked meal. But, then again, the food served in the Morning Glory dining room was usually very good. But tonight she would insist on paying the tab. Ever since she had attended the family gathering at Frank's request, the two of them had had dinner together quite frequently. The usual procedure for dinner was quite informal. Residents would come into the dining room and take a seat at any table they wished. Or, they could ask to join someone else who was seated already. Most of the men were a little bashful when it came to asking the women if they could join them, but the ladies took to this idea very quickly.

Marty had noticed that ever since the prom, the ladies seem to have warmed up to Nigel. They used to pretend that they didn't see him come into the dining room, appearing to be very intent in their own conversation. There were times that Nigel and Rosebud would join her and Frank for dinner. However, this usually made Ellie May look for other dinner partners and Marty was afraid that this sudden pairing off would hurt the bond that the three ladies had formed so easily.

When she spotted Frank standing at the doorway of the dining room, she smiled. He always looked so neat—handsome, in fact. "Hello Frank, right on time I see. I would like to sit at one of the round tables so we can seat more people. I'm concerned that Ellie May might be feeling like a fifth wheel when she comes into the dining room."

"Anywhere you would like, Marty," Frank said as he took Marty's arm. "After all, Ellie May is a friend of yours, and I think she's also a great dinner companion, especially when she talks about the crime stories she watches."

The dining room, with its snowy white tablecloths and colorful centerpieces, was impressive. A large window gave the diners a good view of the maple trees beyond the terrace. "Look, Frank, aren't the trees gorgeous? I love the fall."

"I agree," Frank said. "Here comes Ellie May."

Marty gave Ellie May a little wave and she quickly joined them. "What looks good on the menu tonight? I had the beef last night and it was really tough. I think there is just too much chicken on the menu each night. I'd like to see some good old-fashioned, Pennsylvania Dutch dinners being offered" Ellie May complained.

"I think I'll have the broiled salmon," Marty said.

Just then Rosebud and Nigel walked over to the table and sat down. Nigel leaned over to Ellie May and said, "A lady, in a retirement home in Florida, sitting on a bench enjoying the sunshine, when a gentleman comes out the front door and sits down beside her. 'Are you new here?' she asks. 'Yes, I just checked in yesterday.' 'Oh, where were you before?' 'I was in prison.' 'My, what were you in prison for?' Very nonchalantly, he replies, 'I killed my wife.' The lady then replied rather happily, 'Oh that means you're available.'"

"Not one of your best, Nigel. But I know one woman here who is constantly looking for her next husband. She would probably respond just like the lady in your joke," Ellie May said jokingly to see if she could get a rise out of Nigel. As her attention turned to the server at the next table, Ellie said, "Marty, is the server over there new? She looks familiar."

"That's Hilda. I heard she used to work in the kitchen at *Serenity*," Nigel said.

"Oh, no, not the infamous *Serenity*," Rosebud groaned.

"Did you know it's up for sale?" Nigel asked. "I hear that the owner's wife is going to clean his clock!"

"Well, she should. He was a low-down skunk," Ellie May offered.

"Women always have the upper hand when it comes to property settlement. Just ask William. He went through the wringer four times. And, he better be careful—it could happen again," Nigel said as he laughed.

"Nigel, that's not nice," Rosebud said. "The *Serenity* incident was a case of a man who was even too dumb to cheat and get away with it."

"I have to agree with that," Ellie May said. "One would think that someone smart enough to be a businessman would be smart in other areas."

The dinner conversations evolved into opinions on the meals, the dining room attendance, politics and religion. Even when discussing hot topics, such as politics and religion, they were respectful to one another—a comfort level that felt good.

"Well," Nigel said in an upbeat tone, "I guess we calmly solved the world's problems, don't you think so, Frank?"

Before Frank could respond, Ellie May said, "Uh. Oh. Here comes one of our newest residents—the Colonel. I met him this morning and I am not impressed. He's an egotist and very rude. Maybe we should run for cover. I'm glad we're just about finished with our dinner."

As the new resident stopped in front of their table, he looked them over haughtily as he pushed his glasses up his bulbous nose and said, "May I join you people? I am Colonel Matthew Anderson." Without waiting for anyone's permission, he pulled out a chair and sat down.

"Welcome, Matthew," Nigel said politely.

"I prefer to be called Colonel, if you don't mind," the newcomer stated firmly.

"I can relate to that feeling," Nigel said. "I prefer to be called *Your Royal Highness*."

"Are you trying to be funny, or are you being facetious? That is, if you know what that word means," the colonel said directly to Nigel.

"Tell you what, Matthew, I do know what that word means. The question remains though: If you really knew what *facetious* means, you would not have to ask me." Then, with exaggerated pomp, Nigel gracefully turned to Rosebud and bowed. "Now, my Queen, our imperial presence is requested in the card room where our subjects are awaiting."

Rosebud didn't even try to hide the smile on her face. As she stood up, she said, "Ladies, I'll see you in the morning." Turning to Matthew and using her sweetest tone, she looked at the colonel and said, "Welcome to Morning Glory Hill, *Matthew*."

After a few moments of silence, Marty said, "Colonel Anderson, I think I must explain something to you. A few weeks ago, Nigel was selected as King of our prom. He was just having a little fun with his newly bestowed title."

"I find it abhorrent that so many people don't respect earned titles. I was stupified when I looked over the Morning Glory directory to discover that there are no doctors or anyone with earned titles listed."

"But there *are*. We happen to have three doctors: one is a retired dentist and two are retired professors. In addition, we also have one retired attorney. All of them requested that their titles not be included in the directory," Marty responded patiently.

Colonel Anderson turned his head as he became aware that someone was standing right beside him. When Marty realized Jesse was standing there, she was about to introduce them to one another. However, she stopped short when she saw an angry looked on Jesse's face.

"What's up?" Jessie snapped as she banged her cane sharply on the floor. "So, we meet again, dear Colonel. How sharp is your tongue tonight? Is it as insulting as it was when we bumped into one another this morning in The Square?" Jesse paused for a moment. "My esteemed Colonel, *it isn't polite to be rude, to do otherwise is to be crude.'*" Jessie banged her cane on the floor once again, gave the colonel the cold shoulder, and stomped off, leaving him red-faced with his mouth hanging wide open.

Chapter 36

Becky Johnson, physical therapist for Morning Glory Hill, was standing on the edge of the pool, conducting a water-based cardio exercise. She was pleased that her group had expanded to eighteen women in such a short period of time. Becky was proud of the ladies for coming to class regularly and working so hard to improve their bodies.

Her students especially enjoyed using the Styrofoam barbells—an exercise she had just introduced last week. They weren't nearly as happy when they had to perform jumping-jacks, and while they complained about having to do so many, they all completed the routine. She also had them form various patterns in the pool, requiring them to run back and forth, a great exercise for the legs that was easy to perform. Meanwhile, Jessie was seated on a nearby bench, patiently waiting for her cue from Becky that she could enter the water.

"Now take your positions along the right side of the pool. Jessie, hold my hand as you come down the steps and stand right in front of me. Good. Now, hold on to the edge and kick your feet behind you one at a time. Try to keep in rhythm to the music—that's it—very good. Now turn and put your back against the wall and kick one foot out and then the other."

Becky noted that Jessie was doing well without her cane. The therapist kept a very close eye on her to make certain that Jessie was protected at all times. "Great, Jessie, marvelous."

"Okay, that's it for today. You're all making great progress. While I have you here in front of me, I want to wish Rosebud and her dancing partner good luck tonight at the dance contest in Ringville."

"Thank you," Rosebud said. "We understand that we'll have some stiff competition tonight." Rosebud was thrilled when the women gathered around her, wishing her good luck and showering her with compliments.

As the women filed into the locker room, Rosebud's thoughts shifted to Marty's necklace. She had had an idea that formed ever since she had heard about Hilda and her connection to *Serenity*. "Marty, how about you and Ellie May hanging out here for a few minutes," Rosebud requested.

Eventually, the three were alone. Rosebud then said, "I think we need to befriend Hilda—the new dining room server who used to work at *Serenity*. She might be able to tell us where Susan is. I still think she's the one who has the necklace. We have to be careful how we approach her because Hortense is a stickler when it comes to any staff member getting too familiar with the residents. But, it is possible that she could lead us to Susan. Do you have any suggestions how we could do this?" "How about Marty telling Hilda about her doll collection and offering to let her see it sometime? It sounds very innocent," Ellie May suggested.

"That might work. What do you think, Marty?" Rosebud asked.

"We need to figure a way to get to speak with her without too many other people around. Remember, it's got to look unplanned," Ellie May reminded her friends. "It's a strategy that is often used in crime stories."

"If we knew when Hilda clocks-in, maybe we could find ourselves near the parking lot when she drives in," Rosebud said.

"But what would we be doing in the employee parking lot?" Marty asked.

"What about bumping into her somewhere in the community?" Ellie May offered.

"I'll get on the Internet and see what I can find and then I'll get back to you," Rosebud said. "There has to be a way that we can talk to her without Hortense knowing anything about it. After all, this has nothing to do with Morning Glory Hill."

"Oh, but it does," insisted Ellie May. "Morning Glory Hill is the scene of the crime."

As the three picked up their gym bags and headed out of the pool area, they spotted Colonel Anderson coming out of the men's locker room. "My goodness," Rosebud said, "that man's stomach is just as big as his ego." She purposefully turned her head to let him know that she didn't like him. She couldn't bear to see any more of his saggy body.

Rosebud hurried to her apartment, sat down at her computer, and began searching for information about Hilda. She was almost ready to give up when she stumbled across a link that, at first, appeared to be unrelated. The website for a local food bank appeared on the screen. She paged down a bit, and there it was! Hilda had been recognized as the outstanding volunteer of the month. Rosebud picked up her cell phone. "Marty, I think I found a way that you can meet Hilda off site!"

Chapter 37

Early morning visitors to The Square were delighted to see a table in the center of the room where a large silver trophy was displayed. Hortense wanted all the residents to see the prize that Rosebud and Nigel had won at the dance contest the night before. She thought it would be nice to recognize the dancers before she placed the beautiful silver cup in the trophy case.

By the time Nigel arrived, word had spread about the trophy and The Square was crowded with residents. When he saw what Hortense had done with the trophy, his chest swelled with pride. He hadn't had many successes in his life to brag about, but now that his talent as a dancer was recognized, he was elated. Of course, he had to give Rosebud some of the credit, but deep in his heart, he knew that it was he who guided her across the floor. And, he felt that Rosebud was beginning to see him in a new light—and who knew where that could lead. He wondered if he was too old to be a friend with benefits.

"Nigel, you and Rosebud should go on *Dancing with the Stars*. You could win that, too," Celeste said as she parked her little book-filled wagon.

"We can't do that. But thanks for the compliment," Nigel said.

Suddenly, Rosebud was at his side. "Nigel, wasn't it nice of Hortense to display our trophy?"

"Now you and I don't have to fight over who really owns it," Nigel said. "I guess it really belongs to Morning Glory Hill!" Before Rosebud could agree, Nigel whispered, "Look who's coming."

"Well, well, what have we here?" Colonel Anderson said mockingly as he looked at the engraving on the trophy. "It certainly can't be a trophy for brainpower, now, can it?"

Although Anderson towered over her, Rosebud moved directly in front of him. "Matthew, must you be so damned insulting all the time? Can't you ever say anything nice?" Rosebud said angrily.

"Little lady…"

"Don't you 'little lady' me," Rosebud responded as she wagged her finger at the man. "My name is Rosebud McClaren. I am shocked that someone who claims to be a colonel, demonstrates such a total lack of manners."

"People, people," Hortense said as she tried to calm down the situation. "We are all adults here, so I think we all need to act accordingly."

The colonel stormed off mumbling under his breath and hurriedly went out the front entrance.

"I apologize," Rosebud said, "but, he is insufferable."

"Let's put this incident aside," Hortense said. "Folks, aren't we proud of Rosebud and Nigel?"

The crowd showed their appreciation by applauding.

Rosebud sat down to cool off. She didn't like to get so angry—her mother would be appalled. That thought made her smile. Then again, perhaps her mother would have handled the situation the same way.

"Rosebud, you were terrific!" Nigel said. "I didn't know you had such fire in your belly."

"Nigel, I certainly wouldn't call it that. However, I have had enough of his pomposity. From now on, I'll try to keep my distance from him. He better watch out, though; I *will* get back at him without him ever being the wiser—so help me!"

"Rosebud," Nigel said as he stood up, "you are a very special woman. I'm off to my bowling league now. Please don't murder the good colonel while I'm gone—I would really like to see that."

Chapter 38

Marty was experiencing mixed emotions about her afternoon meeting with Hilda. Yesterday it had seemed perfectly alright and she had had no qualms about the plan that Rosebud, Ellie May and she had hatched to get more information about Susan. Remarkably, she had had an opportunity to speak with Hilda in the dining room last evening and it had gone very well. Hilda was surprised that she knew about the recognition she had received from the food bank. Marty stretched the truth a bit when she told Hilda that the Women's Group of Morning Glory Hill was looking for ways to get more involved in the community and thought perhaps they could help the food bank. Marty stressed that she didn't want to put Hilda's job in jeopardy. Since Hortense was so protective about projects that might involve both staff and residents, Marty thought they should meet off site. Hilda was most gracious and suggested that she could meet Marty at the food bank. Now, however, Marty was feeling very much like a traitor since her main goal was to get information about Susan.

Perhaps Benedict Arnold felt the same way. While this certainly was not a matter of national security, it bordered on intrigue. Marty felt that her necklace was just not worth what she was about to do and perhaps she should just call off the meeting. On the other hand, *if* she could get the necklace back, and *if* it was the real thing, she could help the food bank in a big way. Could this be a case where the end results justified the means?

Just as she was climbing the few steps leading to the office of the food bank, a large truck backed into the driveway. She heard the clanging of the heavy, metal warehouse doors as they were being pulled up. Pausing to observe the scene, Marty watched as two men with hand trucks began moving cartons of what appeared to be canned goods into the facility. Marty decided that she would go ahead and meet with Hilda and, regardless of the outcome, she would help in some way to make sure that trucks like these would continue to roll into the driveway.

Hilda was elated to see Marty. "I'm so glad that you came, Mrs. Miller. Let's go into the meeting room so we can hear each other more clearly. When our trucks are unloading, it can sometimes get quite noisy."

"While I know a little about food banks, I really don't know too much about how they operate, so I would appreciate it if you could give me a quick overview," Marty said.

"Certainly. Normally, a food bank procures food from multiple sources and stores it for eventual distribution to charitable agencies. Think of us as the middlemen—donated food goes to one place where it can then be sorted and shared with food pantries and other agencies that provide food or cooked meals to the needy."

"Amazing. So, the whole process really depends on the generosity of people and the organizational skills of those who run the various agencies," Marty concluded.

"Nonperishable food comes in from many sources. Some of our well-known stores such as Walmart, Target, and Safeway, just to mention a few, are partners. While we do receive funding through grants and from corporations, most of our funding comes from individuals like you," Hilda explained. "We use those funds to purchase foods that we need to fill the nutritional needs of our clients."

"Remarkable," Marty said.

"Many times, people are faced with choosing whether to feed their families, or pay for the other needs in life. So, Marty, we'll be grateful for whatever your club decides to do for us," Hilda said graciously.

Now that gnawing started again. Marty could feel it in her stomach and she was beginning to get a headache. She was certain that her guilty conscience was rattling her brain.

"Hilda, do you have time to go to lunch with me? I'd really like to get to know you better," Marty asked hopefully.

It wasn't long before the two were seated in a small, local Italian restaurant. "I guess it was hard on you when they closed *Serenity*," Marty said.

"It was a shock to all of us. While most of us knew what was happening between our boss and that hussy, we were surprised that the place closed. You know, I really shouldn't call her names—after all, it took two to do what they did," Hilda said sadly.

"Whatever happened to Susan?" Marty asked.

"I'm really not sure. Someone said the other day that she was back in town, but I don't know if that is true. I know that she had family in Ringville, but I don't know if she's there. I lost my job because of her shenanigans. My life was turned upside down. But I'll manage," Hilda said.

"Hilda, I'll get back to you about how Morning Glory Hill can help the food bank. I thank you for taking the time to meet with me. If you hear anything more about Susan, please let me know," Marty said. "You see, she and I have some unfinished business."

Chapter 39

Harvey and Harry were sitting in the gazebo, enjoying the mild fall evening. Harry had been working all day on his photos, trying to decide if any of them were unique enough for him to enter in the November contest. He didn't have too much time to waste since all entries were due by mid-October. Feeling dejected—as if he had really missed the mark this time—Harry had been particularly despondent for days. Harvey had finally convinced Harry to take a break.

"I'm glad you suggested this," Harry said. "I apologize for being such a bear lately."

"Not to worry," Harvey said. "I have a question for you. How many stars can you see?"

Harry chuckled. "Are you kidding?"

"Got you to smile, didn't I?" Harvey said, pleased with his results.

"Mind if we join you?" Gordon asked as he held on to Marie's hand.

"Come on in," Harvey said. "We're just sitting here counting the stars."

"Don't mind him, folks," Harry said. "Harvey's trying to get me out of a snit, and I think it's working."

"It's such a romantic evening," Marie said. "I'm not certain that I'm good at counting stars, but I'm willing to try," she said in a voice that was as soft as velvet.

"I just wanted Harry to think of anything other than his photos. It's contest time and he feels like he hasn't captured a winning photo, yet."

"Maybe you already have one," Marie suggested.

"No, I don't think so. Something is missing, but I can't put my finger on it," Harry tried to explain. "I haven't captured something that I feel is unique."

"Speaking about unique, I've been meaning to ask you: Are they cyclamens that you have in that brass planter on your porch in front of your bay window? They are such a beautiful shade of red," Marie said.

"Yes, they are; not wild ones, though. I got them from different florists," Harvey answered.

"Do they bloom all year round?" Marie asked.

"Mine will have flowers through the winter, but the plants will be dormant during the summer. There are many kinds of cyclamen plants and they come in a variety of colors," Harvey said. "I'm not sure that they will continue to bloom much longer. It seems that something has been disturbing the ground in the pot."

"It might be a raccoon," Marie suggested.

"You know they eat almost anything, but they also fancy the worms and bugs around the roots of plants," Gordon added.

"Harry that could be it!" Harvey said excitedly. "If there is a raccoon interested in those plants, he probably only comes around at night. How about hooking up a motion sensitive camera and maybe you could catch the little rascal that's messing with our plants."

"Oh, what a precious photo that would make, Marie said. "Perhaps even a winning one!"

"I love nature. While we don't have much ground to grow things, I do my best to bring the outside into our home," Harvey said.

"Have you ever tried growing morning glories? I never have had much luck with them," Marie asked.

"I haven't planted them here, but in our previous place I had them in the back yard. There are morning glories that bloom only at night; they're called moonflowers," Harvey explained. "But if you'd like to try planting morning glories near your patio, I'd be glad to give you a hand."

"Why, thank you, Harvey," Marie said graciously. "You know, it is so peaceful here. We get little noise from the traffic, and we have a glorious view morning and night."

Gordon took his wife's hand, and said, "Just look up there, Marie—look at that astonishing display." He turned to face Harry and Harvey. "It is such a delight to be with good friends who also enjoy reveling in the beauty of Mother Nature. We're all quite fortunate to be here at Morning Glory Hill."

The four of them grew quiet. There was no need for any more words. The beauty of the night spoke volumes.

Chapter 40

Marty and Frank arrived early at The Square to prepare for the Morning Glory Hill Food Drive. Preston helped them set up four, long folding tables so they could arrange the food donations for all to see.

"Frank, I brought my dad's old cigar box for us to use for cash or check donations. We may not have a fancy cash box, but it will suffice. Look, the price on the box says the cigars were only five cents."

"I never smoked cigars," Frank said. "But I used to indulge in chewing tobacco when I was working my farm."

"Ugh," Marty said. "I'm glad you don't do that anymore. Thanks for bringing all those empty cartons. We'll need them when we get things ready for the food bank to pick up. Here come some donations now," Marty said when she spotted a group of residents carrying tote bags and heading their way.

Ever since her visit with Hilda at the food bank the other day, Marty had felt bad; almost traitorous. To try to make herself feel better, she vowed that she would make it up to Hilda by making sure that Morning Glory Hill would, indeed, have a productive food drive. She had prepared fliers that she took to each apartment, and she had made personal contact with as many of the residents as she could, making certain they understood that the food bank not only needed nonperishables, but also money to meet the hunger needs of the people in the area.

"Marty," Colonel Anderson said loudly, as he worked his way to the front of the crowd, "I hope that you will accept my check in lieu of canned goods. You see, I have no need for groceries in my apartment. I either eat out, or I go to our dining room," the pompous man said as he dramatically laid the check on the table face up, so others standing around might see that it was for $500.

"Colonel Anderson, thank you very much," Marty said as she casually placed the check inside the cigar box. "I'm certain that others will benefit from your generosity."

Celeste, who had been pulling her little red wagon behind her, stopped alongside the colonel and said, "Marty, I've got a nice load of groceries here. My sister helped me fill my wagon with all kinds of good food."

"How nice of her," Marty said. "I think we should make her an honorary resident."

"Oh, that's right, she also gave me a check," Celeste said as she rummaged through her Vera Bradly purse. "It's in here somewhere— here it is," she said gleefully as she pulled a check from her bag. "Sorry, it's a bit crumpled, but it's still okay."

Colonel Anderson, looking over the top of his glasses said, "I hope you don't treat all your money that way, my dear woman."

"Thanks for calling me *dear*, Matthew," Celeste said as she bestowed her sweetest smile on the irritated man. "That's the nicest thing you have ever said to me," she said as she turned and walked away, pulling her wagon behind her and smiling broadly.

William and Abigail were hurrying across The Square with several bags in their arms. "Marty, we wanted to be certain that we gave you our groceries and our checks," William said as he handed the bags to Frank. "We can't stay to help since we have a music program we're putting on for the seniors at Huntington Heights."

"Thank you so much," Marty said. "I know that the seniors will be thrilled with your program," Marty said as she added the envelopes to the cigar box.

Marty couldn't help but notice how happy Abigail seemed to be. She watched as the two of them, walking hand in hand, disappeared out the front door. She took a moment to look at Frank He looked very handsome with his sweater vest and paisley cotton shirt. He was sorting the cans and making an impressive display for the residents to look at. How could it have happened that in a short period of time, he had come to mean so much to her? She would have to be careful. After all, they certainly weren't teenagers. But she couldn't deny that, when Frank stood alongside of her or when he held a chair for her in the dining room, she felt like one.

As residents approached the tables with bags of groceries, Rosebud and Ellie May unpacked the bags and handed the items to Frank. The tables were slowly filling up with a cornucopia of foodstuffs, all neatly arranged. Jessie was walking back and forth, checking out the labels and shaking her head back and forth.

"Is something wrong, Jessie?" Rosebud asked.

"No. I am just amazed at the variety of things on these tables. I'm so proud of our residents. Marty, this was a great idea. You are such a kind person," Jessie said.

"Thanks, Jessie. But you're right about our residents. They came through with flying colors," Marty said. She wondered what Jessie would have said if she knew why she had gone to the food bank in the first place. The only thing going through Marty's mind at the moment was guilt—burdensome, oppressive guilt.

Marty jumped when Frank said, "Marty, Hortense told me that Morning Glory Hill has prepared a check for your food drive. How about I ask her to come over with the check so we can take her picture as she is presenting it to you?" Frank suggested.

"That's a great idea," Marty replied. As Frank walked away, her thoughts returned to Frank. For some reason, she told herself, when Frank was around, her heart beat a bit faster and her steps were lighter. Maybe she's coming down with something—or maybe not.

But suddenly her thoughts shifted to the dark side. Now she was beginning to feel guilty once again. She had gotten involved in the food bank drive by trying to get information about Susan and that stupid necklace. She hoped that she would be forgiven for not sharing all this with Frank. He's bound to find out some time. Perhaps later, she might confess her lack of honesty to Frank—just not today. She hadn't lied to Hilda since she does have unfinished business with Susan. But then, why does she feel like a liar?

After the photo session was over, they decided to count the number of cans and boxes. When they had the final total, they were pleased that the residents had contributed 724 items.

As they all began packing the groceries in cartons, Preston reminded them not to make them too heavy. "Remember, ladies, don't try to lift them. I'll get them with the hand truck and Frank and I will take everything to the backdoor on Blossom Road. There's plenty of room back there for the food truck."

"Marty, I can drive some of you to the food bank, if you'd like," Frank offered. "You might want to take some pictures there, too."

"Great. Rosebud, why don't you and Ellie May go along with Frank and me? I'm certain that we will enjoy seeing all the items we have gathered being placed on the shelves at the food bank," Marty said.

"I'll get my car and I'll meet you out front," Frank said as he scurried away.

"Wow, we received $450 in cash, and...are you ready for this?" Marty asked. "We took in a whopping $5,750 in checks!" Marty didn't mention that Frank had donated $4000 in honor of his four daughters. She was certain that Frank wouldn't want the others to know. It would be a secret—just between the two of them. She really liked that idea.

Chapter 41

Harvey was busy preparing breakfast while Harry finished dressing. Harry had been a bit grumpy lately and that was not his usual demeanor. Harvey knew better than to pressure Harry into telling him what was wrong. Harry would eventually share his concerns—but in his own time. While he knew Harry felt that none of his latest photographs were good enough to submit to the contest, Harvey hoped that that was all his husband was worried about. Even when Harvey put a plateful of waffles and bacon in front of him, Harry said nothing. As soon as Harry finished his meal, he got up and went out the front door to check on the camera he had placed there to catch whatever was eating Harvey's cyclamen plants.

Suddenly, Harry ran back into their apartment, waving his camera in the air. "I think we caught him," Harry said excitedly. "I hope we got at least one good picture of the cyclamen thief!" Harry said as he flopped on the sofa to examine his camera.

Harvey was waiting to hear who the thief was. But, he couldn't imagine what Harry found on his camera since he was sitting perfectly still, staring at the camera in disbelief.

"What is it—a raccoon—a groundhog?" Harvey asked hopefully.

"You'll never guess. A rather large, unsavory creature," Harry responded.

"C'mon now, Harry. Are you saying your camera caught a monster?"

"Exactly," Harry said. "Come over here and look."

Harvey sat down beside Harry and leaned over to look at the camera screen. He was confused. It was no creature from the fields. It was Samuel Long, President of the Morning Glory Hills Council. "I...I don't understand," was all Harvey could get out.

"That bastard was spying on us! What he expected to find I'm not sure. But now we know he's certainly not our friend. That rotten, no-good SOB was probably watching us for some time now. Who knows how long this was going on? He probably was kneeling on the cement and holding on to your brass planter with his hands. That's what disturbed the dirt around the cyclamens. He never thought that a camera would catch him. I hope he peed his pants when he heard the camera clicking."

"What are we going to do?" Harvey asked. "Should we report this to Hortense?"

Harry paced back and forth, all the while holding his camera and smiling. Finally, he said, "Oh, I have no intention of reporting this to Hortense. That would be too easy. I'm going to get back at him for this. I am going to kill him with kindness and Oscar will help me."

"You can't hurt Oscar!" Harvey said as he put his hands over his mouth.

"Of course not. He loves that cat, but unfortunately, I like Oscar, too," Harry said as he sat down at his desk. "Hmmm, I need to be clever. This is no time to fly off the handle. I could rant and rave and scare the crap out of him. But, I want to have some fun with him. I want him to think that there is a sword hanging over his gray head all the time. I know. I will be so nice to him that he will be scared all the time."

Harvey knew better than to interrupt Harry when he got like this. He was certain that Samuel would rue the day that he messed with Harry. This was really going to be fun.

"I've got it!" Harry said sharply. "I'll call on Samuel today. I'll be extremely nice to him as I ask whether or not he will give me permission to photograph Oscar for the contest. That'll confuse him. He undoubtedly heard the clicking of the camera. But when he sees that I am not angry, he won't be certain any longer that the noise he heard *was* a camera. I'm hoping that he thinks he got away with spying on us. But, I'll drop him little clues that might shake his confidence."

"I know he's an egotist, so do you really think you can pull this off?" Harvey asked.

"Oscar will pull it off for me. If he thinks that his beloved Oscar might be the subject of a winning photo in a magazine, it'll work. I'll take some props along and shoot dozens of photos, and I'll have little old Samuel in my hip pocket. One day, when the timing is right, this photo," Harry said as he pointed to the screen on his camera, "will show up some place where he'll least expect it. Then, he'll know for certain that I played him big time."

Chapter 42

Samuel hadn't slept at all during the night. Now, as he looked into the mirror, he could see that his eyes were bloodshot and his face appeared haggard. While he couldn't be certain that he had heard a camera clicking as he peered into the Hamilton's living room—and he wanted desperately to be believe that he had not been captured on film—he couldn't stop thinking about the consequences that he might have to face for his stupid act. He certainly couldn't go to Harry and confess—totally out of the question. He had even thought about quickly moving out of Morning Glory Hill, but scratched that idea as foolish. Samuel resolved that he would have to face it like a man and take whatever his fate would be.

Oscar, on the other hand, was quite content. He was curled up on his favorite pillow as his blue eyes followed Samuel's every move. "You are lucky, Oscar. I take care of you and I shield you from any harm. I have no protector," Samuel said as he took a moment to pet Oscar. "Oscar, what if I visit Harry, confess what I did, and ask for forgiveness?" Oscar simply closed his eyes.

Samuel knew that he would not confess anything at all to Harry. But he didn't know how he would tolerate Harry at the next poker game. Then, another horrible thought entered his mind. What would he do if Harry told everyone what he caught on his camera? And, perhaps he would even show them the picture. What would his defense be? Stupid. Stupid. Stupid. If only he hadn't spied on them that night. If only—well, *if only* died—he had spied and he had been caught.

He had to get away for a while. Perhaps he could visit one of his old buddies and forget about this mess for a short time. When he was with them, he didn't have to worry about being *politically correct*. Samuel wouldn't be surprised if the government found a way to get into people's minds and tell them what to say and to whom. Just as he was about to take his jacket out of the closet, his doorbell rang.

When he saw that his visitor was Harry, he almost fainted. Harry had several cameras slung over his shoulders and was carrying a large canvas bag. When Samuel saw a smile on Harry's face, he relaxed a bit. "Harry, what can I do for you?" he asked apprehensively.

"I've come to ask for a favor. I don't know if I told you before, but I want to enter the photo contest that is being sponsored by the National Photographers Society, and I would like your permission to focus on Oscar."

For a few seconds, Samuel was speechless. When he regained his composure, he said, "Why that would be great. Oscar is a beauty and we would love to help you win the contest," Samuel said as he tried to control the quiver in his voice.

"Great. I brought some props along to see if Oscar is curious about any of them," Harry said.

Samuel picked up Oscar from his pillow and said, "Where would you like to start, Harry?"

"Let's put some of these props on the floor and let Oscar investigate them," Harry said.

Oscar seemed particularly curious about a bright, orange-colored plastic sieve. Harry was able to get a few shots before Oscar lost interest.

"I need something that will show off Oscar's beautiful coat. Let's take Oscar down to Hannah's sanctuary and see how we can take advantage of the serene setting there to show him off. And, we might be able to capture the beauty of both the morning glory garden and Oscar."

"Okay," a relieved Samuel responded. He was beginning to feel that he had nothing to fear from Harry. Maybe he had imagined that clicking sound.

"I would also like to get a shot of Oscar in the library, if you don't mind," Harry said.

"That's fine with me and I'm sure Oscar will love all the attention," Samuel said, smiling for the first time.

They stopped at the library first. Harry removed some of the books to make room for Oscar. "Put Oscar here, Samuel." Harry was having a delightful time, ordering Samuel around and watching the man bend over backwards to please him.

As they entered Hannah's Meditation Room, Harry said, "Samuel, there's the perfect spot for Oscar—the morning glory garden. His coat, against the purple, pink, and blue colors of the morning glories, will look amazing. Wait. I need to get something out of my bag," Harry said as he retrieved a pair of wire-rimmed glasses.

Samuel put Oscar down on the silk flowers. "Here, Samuel, put these on him," Harry ordered.

Oscar was a perfect model. He apparently loved the attention and was totally relaxed. As Harry looked through the lens, he saw what could easily be an award-winning photo: The vibrant colors of the morning glories, Oscar's shimmering silver fur, and his piercing blue eyes, looking over the top of wire-rimmed glasses could mean a winner for Harry.

"That's it, Samuel. I appreciate your cooperation. I know we have several excellent shots, but the last one probably will be the best," Harry explained.

"I can't wait until I see your finished work, Harry. You certainly are a professional photographer. I'm sure we have a prize picture," Samuel said eagerly.

"Well, Samuel, you know what they say about pictures—one picture is worth a thousand words," Harry said as he walked away.

Those words reverberated in Samuel's ears like thunder during an early morning storm.

Chapter 43

Ellie May had been baking all morning. She sank into her soft leather chair and reached for the remote. Perhaps she would find some reruns of the crime shows she loved to watch. She had to admit that she had seen some of these several times. But, with each viewing, she would learn a bit more about the investigative process. She expected Marty and Rosebud would arrive before too long to join her for coffee and cookies. The aroma in her apartment was sweet enough to draw any cookie-lover to her doorstep.

She had set her table with her best china and the linen napkins that her grandmother had made. Ellie May was pleased with the result. She missed the times when she cooked dinners for up to twenty people and fussed for days over what she would serve and who she would seat by whom. Her cooking was the envy of all her friends. Ellie May knew that she wouldn't win any beauty contest, but she did know that she could out-cook any woman in Morning Glory Hill. Now she had two loves—cooking and detective stories. She often wondered if there was a way that she could combine both of those loves, but so far, she hadn't found a solution.

Ellie May also loved her family, especially her three sons who were her pride and joy. One was an executive with the local chocolate company, another was a disc jockey for WDMD, and the third, her baby, owned an automobile repair shop. And, as far as looks was concerned, they all took after their dad—tall, dark and handsome. When she would share her thoughts with her sons about the murder mysteries that she loved so much, they would laugh. Her boys always had their noses glued to the television for any kind of sports that she found boring. Ellie May was certain that if *Tidley Winks* became a sport, they would watch that, too.

Just as Ellie May looked up at the clock, the door opened and her friends came rushing into the kitchen.

"My God, Ellie May, the aroma of peanut butter cookies fills the hallway. You're going to be swamped with hungry visitors," Rosebud warned. "Oh, my. The table is beautiful! You must be expecting someone very important."

"Yes, but they're coming later," Ellie May teased.

It didn't take the ladies long to dig into the scrumptious cookies. Their conversation covered a range of subjects—from the weather, to the new residents. "Now that you have your tummies full and we covered all the usual topics, I have exciting news for the both of you."

"I know," Marty said, "you solved another *Dateline* murder mystery before the end of the show."

"Oh, go on," Ellie May deadpanned, "I do that all the time. No, this is really news. I would have told you yesterday, but you two were busy running around heaven-knows-where. To punish you, perhaps I should just keep this news to myself."

"You knew that we went on that museum tour. We had invited you to go along, but you refused since you had some shows to watch. So, come on, what's the news?" Rosebud asked anxiously.

"I know where Susan is," Ellie May said softly. It felt like a bomb had been dropped.

Marty dropped her cookie and Rosebud almost choked on her coffee. "What!" they said in unison.

"You heard right—Susan—I found her," a self-satisfied Ellie May said smugly.

Rosebud put her hand over her mouth. Marty just stared at Ellie May, all the while shaking her head in disbelief.

"I was in the *Save Money* store yesterday to pick up some of the granola that I like—you know, *Grumpy Bear Granola*—it's hard to find since it's always hidden away on the bottom shelf—I really don't know why. Well, anyway, I was leaning over, hanging on to my shopping cart since I had vertigo, when I was almost run over with a flat truck loaded with cartons. Suddenly, this woman was alongside me, apologizing for scaring me. I opened my mouth to speak, but when I saw that it was Susan, no words came out right away. She was very polite and said she was just getting used to the electronic flat truck. It was then that she recognized me and seemed flustered."

"Susan, stacking shelves? I can't believe that," Rosebud said.

"I'm not exactly sure what I said then, but I told her I was surprised to see her. She told me that she had to move out of Kensington Place since the apartment had been leased for only three months. Almost in a whisper, she said that she had been a complete fool and that Fredrick had played her as well as his wife. I do remember she said that she was broke and was grateful that she had been hired by *Save Money*."

"I know people will say that she deserves what she got, but I do feel sorry for her," Rosebud said. "Marty, she can't have your necklace if she is really penniless."

"I think you're right," Marty said as she rolled her eyes and sighed. All three were quiet as they digested the news. Then Marty finally said, "I guess the search for that damned necklace is over. I have no idea who really has it. Frankly, I really don't care anymore. I didn't want my son to know about it anyway. He adored his father and I never wanted to put any doubt in his mind about why he had it in his Dopp kit. So, let's consider this *necklace thing* over and get on with our lives."

"Marty, you're a trouper. Perhaps we should accept Susan for what she is—in my mind, at least, a silly young woman who fell for a glib line of a no-good bastard," Rosebud said. "Just wipe it from your mind, Marty, and keep hanging on to the pleasant memories you have of Charlie."

"I'm a bit sad," Ellie May said. "Your missing necklace has brought such excitement to this place. It will really be dull now without any kind of scandal lurking in the background."

"You always have your murder mysteries," teased Rosebud.

"I do have some happy news," Marty said. "My grandson's wife Laura, and little Gretchen, will be back in the States before Thanksgiving. I think I told you that she's been substituting for a woman who was teaching English in a Christian school in Thailand. While Laura said that she loved the assignment in Thailand, she'll be happy to be home again. It seems almost impossible that it was three years ago that we lost my grandson, but I'm grateful that Laura stays in touch with me."

"You can think of Gretchen as a little diamond that your grandson would be happy to share with you," Rosebud said tenderly. "After all, things sometimes lose their importance, but family—well, they're with you forever—no matter where you go."

"I'm looking forward to sitting on my bed with Gretchen again and playing with my dolls. I've missed her. She brings such joy into my life. I can see my grandson in so many of the things she does. She has his high cheek bones and his fine blonde hair. And, when she laughs, I hear him. Did I tell you that Frank made a remarkable two-story dollhouse for Gretchen? She'll love it," Marty said proudly. "It will be a delightful gift."

"You know what? Now that we don't have a mystery to solve, maybe we could make up one of our own," Ellie May suggested.

"Heavens, no!" Marty said. "We'll have to learn to live quiet, uneventful lives like our male residents do—or will that simply be too boring?"

Chapter 44

Marty was on her way to meet Fanny Tower, a new resident. The only information she had on Fanny was that she was from Delaware and decided to live at Morning Glory Hill to be closer to her son. Rosebud had seen some of the items that had been carried out of the moving van and into the apartment on Orchid Lane and, according to her, they were all high-line pieces.

Pressing the doorbell, Marty hoped that she was dressed properly to meet Fanny. Her two-piece suit had been tailored for her last fall and it still looked like it was new. Marty was a firm believer in making a good first impression on anyone—you never knew where a new friendship might go. When Fanny opened the door, Marty was immediately impressed—no jeans and sweatshirts for this fashion plate. "You must be Marty," Fanny said as she extended her hand. Marty got a brief look at some large rings that sparkled almost as radiantly as Fanny's beautiful green eyes. While she was small in stature, Fanny seemed to dominate the room with her presence.

"Hello, Mrs. Tower. I'm so happy to meet you," Marty said graciously.

"Please, call me Fanny," Fanny said as she ushered Marty into her elegant living room.

As Marty looked around, she said, "Fanny, this room is gorgeous. It's hard to believe that you moved in only yesterday. Everything looks perfect."

Fanny laughed. "Oh, I didn't do any of the work. I hired a mover as well as a stager. I just stayed out of their way and that made us all happy."

The two of them spent almost an hour discussing Morning Glory Hill and how Fanny might play a role in some of the activities. Fanny kept wiggling her fingers and her diamonds made an impressive sight. Marty couldn't help but notice her perfectly manicured nails and her stylish wardrobe. Apparently, she was no stranger to Botox. Everything about Fanny screamed money. Marty said, "Fanny, tell me a little something about yourself."

"I'm a widow. My third husband, Peter, passed away almost two years ago. At that time, I had been living in Delaware and I wasn't sure where I wanted to spend the rest of my years, no matter what the number will be. It took a while for me to make that decision, but I finally settled on Morning Glory Hill to be closer to my son. People are usually surprised when they discover that I was married three times."

"We have one gentleman living here who was married four times," Marty said laughingly.

"I always maintain that my first husband gave me my two wonderful children. My second husband gave me a car. But my third husband gave me my money," Fanny said happily. "I've been looking at the directory for Morning Glory Hill and I have a few questions to ask you about some of the residents," Fanny said as she started paging through the directory. "I see that Colonel Matthew Anderson is one of the residents."

"Not very friendly, though," Marty cautioned.

"Oh," Fanny said, obviously disappointed. "Well, is Frank Snyder the Snyder who used to own a large dairy farm? Seems I remember my son dating one of Snyder's daughters a long time ago."

Why, yes. Frank did own a dairy farm," Marty said proudly.

"Now, this place is beginning to become a bit more interesting," Fanny said as she put a circle around Frank's name in the directory.

Marty was dumbfounded. She watched as Fanny seemed lost in her own thoughts.

"Maybe, just maybe, this could be husband number four," Fanny said with a broad smile on her face. "Oh my, look, he lives right here on Orchid Lane!"

Marty couldn't remember how she had gotten out of Fanny's apartment. But she could not deny the sinking feeling that she was experiencing in the pit of her stomach.

Chapter 45

Samuel hadn't been sleeping very well ever since the night he peeked into the window of Harry and Harvey's living room. He kept telling himself that maybe the noise he had heard that night was not the click of a camera, but some random sound of the night. But it was the way that Harry had looked at him when they were taking pictures of Oscar. *One picture is worth a thousand words.* Samuel heard that statement over and over. It seemed to permeate his very psychic. Try as he might, he couldn't shake the feeling of doom. He felt that Harry was planning something—something diabolical.

Deciding that he had to put up a good front—at least until he knew if Harry had any incriminating evidence—Samuel vowed to put all his energy into heading up Morning Glory's Casino Night. Perhaps if he immersed himself in charity work, he might find some peace of mind. After all, the book he had been working on would not use the actual names of anyone here at Morning Glory Hill. It would be a parody, anyway. However, to be safe, he had already deleted all references to a same-sex couple. Damn. Whatever happened to the right to publish his own thoughts and ideas on how people should or should not conduct themselves? This damned politically correct garbage made him angry. Wait a minute—he could still win this battle. Using veiled references and innuendoes, he could get his points across. *That* would show them.

While the Children's Hospital Committee would be responsible for setting up the gaming tables and running the various games for casino night, Samuel would need volunteers to help decorate the dining room and that meant that he would need Harvey.

"Oh, Oscar, you are so lucky that you don't have to pretend to like people. You simply ignore everyone, except for when you're hungry," Samuel said as he gently stroked Oscar's back. As Samuel thought about his predicament, he began to grow angrier. How dare that upstart Harry torment him this way? Here I am, far more educated than that…man—I should be the one to lead him around by his nose. I need to control my own destiny and I will not let Harry Hamilton destroy that.

"Oscar, I must calm down. I must use my mind—my intellect. I can beat this thing. So what if he has a photograph of me peering into that damned window? I should simply laugh it off. But all this is happening at an inconvenient time. Just as I am about to teach a course in history at the university, this had to happen. I don't need to have my personal views blasted all over town. It's all Harry's fault."

As he was lost in his thoughts, Samuel jumped when the phone rang. "Hello," he said rather grumpily.

"Harry here. How about joining me for lunch at *Sassy's*? I have photos to show you."

Samuel wasn't certain that he would be able to speak. His throat was dry and his heart was beating rapidly. "Why...why I would be delighted," he finally said.

"Fine. I'll see you there at noon," Harry said.

Samuel sat there for a moment, holding onto the phone. While he wanted to see the photos, he knew that having lunch in the deli was just another step in Harry's plan to torture him.

Chapter 46

Ellie May was worried about Marty. For the past few days, Marty had not been herself. She appeared to be distracted and distant and that surely was not the Marty that Ellie May knew. She expressed her concern to Rosebud over the phone that morning. Rosebud suggested that they meet with Marty to see if they could ferret out what was going on. Rosebud was afraid that perhaps Marty was having some kind of physical ailment that she didn't want to share with anyone. If that was the case, Rosebud cautioned that they shouldn't be too abrupt when questioning her about her demeanor.

"Remember," Rosebud had said, "let her tell us what's wrong without making her feel uncomfortable. We both know that something is not right, but we must not make her feel guilty in any way."

Elli May made a pan of brownies and set her kitchen table. Perhaps the aroma of the baked goods and the sight of a pretty table would help make Marty feel better. Ellie May believed that good food and friendship could go a long way in helping people change their attitude. Then, Ellie May began to wonder if she had said something, or did something that had hurt Marty. Or maybe someone else did.

By the time her guests arrived, Ellie May had herself worked into a high state of concern. When the thought crossed her mind that Frank might be at the center of the problem, she tried to toss that idea away. Ellie May was never too good at giving people advice about their relationships. While she and her husband had a good marriage, Ellie May had often longed for more passion. She still blushed whenever this thought crossed her mind.

"Oh, good," Marty said as she sat down at the table and spied the brownies. "Just what the doctor ordered."

When Ellie May heard the word *doctor,* she shuddered.

"Marty, how did your meeting with the new resident go? I watched as they carried her furniture in. She has some expensive pieces," Rosebud said. "And, wow, the number of garment bags I saw could choke a cow."

"She is an interesting lady," Marty replied cautiously.

"What's she like?" Ellie May asked.

Marty hesitated. "She seems very...nice. Dresses extremely well and has elegant manners."

Rosebud instinctively dug deeper. "And? Come on, Marty, give us the scoop."

"She told me that she had been married three times. And then she began asking me some strange questions about some of our male residents. That made me a bit uncomfortable," Marty said.

"Like what kind of questions?" Rosebud said.

"She wanted to know what kind of man the colonel is. I told her that he wasn't very friendly. Then she asked about Frank."

"Frank?" both women asked in unison.

"She wanted to know if he was the Snyder that used to own a large dairy farm. She then said that one of her sons used to date one of his daughters."

"What did she say then?" Rosebud pressed.

"What she said next shocked me. She seemed proud when she told me that her first husband had given her children, her second had given her a car, and her third had given her money. She said that this place was getting more interesting and then she circled Frank's name in the directory. Then...then she said that perhaps he could be husband number four," Marty said as she pinched her lips together. "You know they both live on Orchid Lane."

Rosebud was the first to respond. She took Marty's hand in hers and said, "Marty, you have nothing to worry about when it comes to Frank. It's obvious that he adores you."

"Wait a minute," Marty said. "I have no claims on Frank. We are dear friends, but he is free to have other friendships. I don't own the man. While we do have a special friendship, I'm not sure either one of us wants to take it any further."

"I hear you," Rosebud said softly. "Look, Marty, we're your friends. We know that you and Frank are indeed special to one another, and we don't think that will change even with a hundred Fanny Towers."

Marty smiled. "I guess I've been acting like a schoolgirl. Jealousy certainly does not belong in my vocabulary. For heaven's sake, I'm too old to do battle over a man."

"That's my girl," Ellie May said. "But, if we were in a school yard, Rosebud and I would beat the beegeebers out of that Fanny. I just might rip every single hair off her head."

"Who says we still can't do that?" Rosebud said jokingly.

Marty laughed hard. "What on earth would I do without you?"

"Now, why don't you wrap some of these brownies up and take them to Frank?" Ellie May suggested.

"Am I supposed to tell him that I baked them?" Marty asked.

"That's fine with me," Ellie May said.

As Marty walked out the door, she turned and said, "Thanks, ladies. I'll try to keep my head on straight when it comes to Fanny. However, if I ever need a *hitman,* I know who to call."

After the door closed behind Marty, Ellie May said, "Look, Rosebud, we need to keep a close eye on that Fanny. She may be used to getting whatever she wants wherever she goes, but here at Morning Glory Hill, she'll have eyes on her all the time—you and me! I saw a story the other night where this lady..."

"Ellie May, we live in the real world, not a TV show. I agree, we need to watch her like a hawk, but, if she steps out of line, then what do we do?"

Ellie May laughed. "Well, then, I guess we'll have to hire a real hitman!"

Chapter 47

Celeste was pulling her little red wagon, filled with books that she was delivering to residents. She decided that she would stop by the new resident's apartment to find out if Morning Glory Hill had another book-lover in its midst. As she rang the bell, Celeste could hear music coming from behind closed doors. As Fanny opened the door, Celeste said friendly, "Good morning. I'm Celeste Mayfair, volunteer librarian."

"Come in, come in," Fanny encouraged. "Nice to meet you, Celeste."

Celeste immediately felt uncomfortable. The room was elegant—way over the top—lots of gold everywhere. Tall lamps on either side of the pure white satin sofa almost took her breath away. An exquisite oriental rug seemed to set the stage for three occasional side chairs that held gold braided pillows. A wall-to-ceiling bookcase took command of the far wall of the living room. But, when she spied the books, she began to relax a bit.

"I see you are a bibliophile," Celeste said nervously.

"I love to read. But, I must confess, most of the books you see over there represent my late husband's vast collection of rare books. I was tempted to sell them, but I couldn't let them go. They were his pride and joy. Besides, they really make my bookcase look impressive, don't you think?" Fanny remarked as she motioned for Celeste to sit down.

Celeste was taken aback with Fanny's remark, so she deliberately switched the conversation. "I don't know if you're familiar with the various programs that we offer regarding books and the love of reading. In addition to the library in The Square, we have nooks located on each lane where I place a variety of books for residents to borrow. All we ask is that you return them to one of the nooks, or you may give them to me when I deliver books that you may have requested. But, with your collection, you may not need any additional reading materials."

"While I have read many of them, some represent topics that my husband was interested in, not me," Fanny explained as she pushed her glasses higher up on her nose.

"If there is a book you would like to read, just fill out one of the request cards located in each nook and I'll try to get it for you," Celeste said proudly.

"What great service," Fanny replied.

"I deliver lots of books to your neighbor, Frank Snyder. Have you met him yet?"

"No, but I'm certain that we'll meet before too long. What types of books does Frank enjoy?" Fanny asked innocently.

"Oh, he loves non-fiction. He's especially interested in American history. He visits Gettysburg frequently. I know he also attends reenactments of the Civil War that are held nearby. He especially likes books about Abraham Lincoln. I'll leave you this library card that explains our few rules. Just fill it out and put it in the box provided in the book nook," Celeste explained.

After Celeste left the apartment, Fanny walked over to the bookcase, slid the door open to the collection on the bottom shelf, and ran her hands over the gold-edged trim around the three- volume set perched on the shelf. She took them out carefully and placed them on the coffee table. She remembered how pleased her husband had been when he had added these manuscripts about Abraham Lincoln to his collection. She sat down on the sofa and began paging through the books. The photographs of the sixteenth President of the United States were extremely well done and the books were in excellent condition. These would be her ticket to get Frank's attention. Then, who knows where it would go from here. If, as Dr. Phil says, *"past behavior often dictates future behavior"* is true, husband number four may be around the corner.

She walked over to the mirror and turned her head from one side to another, critically examining her face. Pleased that she saw no evidence of wrinkles, she smiled. While she was not bankrupt, at least not yet, she needed to look to the future. She enjoyed the finer things of life and that took money. It appeared that pickings here at Morning Glory Hill were ripe—one, a colonel and the other a wealthy retired farmer. Not bad.

Chapter 48

Celeste was pulling her wagon and hurrying across The Square. "Marty, Marty," she called urgently. "I need to speak with you."

Marty and Marie were looking at a fashion magazine, oohing and aahing over photos of the latest runway styles from Paris. As she motioned for Celeste to join them, Marty made room for her on the sofa. "Celeste, sit here."

"Look, if you two have something you need to discuss, I'll see you later, Marty," Marie said graciously.

"No, oh no," Celeste said. "I just want to share some information about our newest resident with Marty. I found out that she is a bibliophile, and I think you should visit her to enroll her in your book club."

There it was again—that feeling in Marty's stomach. "I've met her already and I told her about the book club. But, I'm glad I bumped into you, Celeste. We're moving ahead on making plans for a gigantic book event for late next year. I was asked to form a committee of five or six residents, who would like to be involved in the conference. The committee would be responsible for meeting authors at the airport, driving them to and from the event, and making sure they have everything they need for their participation. Would you be interested?"

"That sounds like a plum assignment. I would love it," Celeste said excitedly.

"Marie, would you like to serve on the committee, too? I thought that you would be the ideal one to plan a cocktail party for the authors," Marty asked hopefully. "You would work jointly with a member from each of the cooperating bookstores. With your finesse handling people, this should be a breeze for you. Others would be involved in a variety of activities, ranging from planning marketing, to working with publishers, to organizing entertainment for the recognition dinner."

"Certainly," Marie said. "I'd love to help out. However, I would like to suggest that you add Abigail to the committee. She's not only a talented woman, but I know that she has some important contacts in the publishing world. And, maybe, this new lady might be another good member since she loves books, too. It will be a great way for her to get to know the rest of us."

"While the event is over a year away, it won't hurt to begin discussing our charge and developing tentative plans. Ladies, how about lunch?" Marty asked.

"I'd love to, but Gordon and I are due at the lawyer's office at one. I don't think I told you, Marty, but I sold the shop," Marie said, with a bit of sadness in her voice.

"It won't be the same without you, Marie," Marty said.

"I'm certain that you will love the new owner. Her name is Julia Eckenroth, and she's from New York. She is an amazing woman. She's served on the boards of several clothing companies, she's completed an apprenticeship with *Mario's Designs*, and she has written a blog on style," Marie stated.

"I'll go to lunch with you, Marty," Celeste said quickly.

As the two of them entered the deli, they spotted Harry, Harvey, and Samuel seated at a table.

Celeste whispered, "What do you get when you mix sweetness with vinegar?"

Marty pulled her eyebrows together and looked lost.

Leaning closer to Marty, Celeste said, "The Hamiltons are genteel people, and that Samuel, well, he's a country unto himself."

"You completely lost me, Celeste," a bewildered Marty said.

"I know that you always think the best of everyone, Marty, but Samuel is not to be trusted. I get an eerie sense about him. Just be careful with him, okay?"

"I appreciate your concern," Marty responded. "Thank you, you are a dear friend."

"Harry and Harvey are upfront and comfortable with their sexuality. Samuel, on the other hand, can hardly contain his dislike for same-sex couples. While he is careful what he says in public, if you watch him carefully, like I do, you can see the distaste in his face," Celeste said earnestly.

Marty had to admit that Celeste was observant and a good judge of character—something that perhaps Marty needed to develop within herself. As Marty picked up the list of specials for the day, she said, "Let's hope that Samuel realizes how he comes across to us and has an epiphany."

"Could be, could be," Celeste said as she turned her head to look at Samuel. "But don't bet on it."

Marty laughed. "Do you know what they say about people who make assumptions?"

"Yeah, I know. But Samuel always looks as if he smells something disgusting when he talks to some people. Be careful with him, Marty, it will take a clever fox to catch him at his game."

Meanwhile, Harry appeared to be enjoying himself immensely. He was smiling, tapping on Samuel's arm like an old buddy, and generally basking in the cleverness of his own scheme.

"This is really nice, Samuel. By the way, do you prefer to be called Samuel, or would you rather I address you as Sam?" Harry asked.

"Oh, it really doesn't matter. Father always called me Sam, but Mother—well, she refused to stop calling me Samuel," Samuel said as cheerfully as he could manage.

"Sam, I have some great news for you and Oscar," Harry said.

"We won the contest?" Samuel asked excitedly.

"The contest has not been announced yet. But this news is just as spectacular. Hortense and the Board of Morning Glory Hill want permission to use the photos of Oscar in their advertisements and brochures. How about that?" Harry said as his chest expanded a bit.

"That's great, Harry! Now everyone will know what an unbelievable beauty he is," Samuel said with pride.

"Hortense wants us to stop by her office so we can sign release forms for the use of Oscar's pictures," Harry said as he patted Samuel on his back. "But, due to contest regulations, we can't do that until the contest is over. I'm also grateful to Oscar for bringing us together," Harry said sincerely. "It's always great to find a new friend. And, if we win the photo contest, you and I will be guests of honor at the next annual association meeting. Won't that be fun?"

Chapter 49

All afternoon, truck after truck had been pulling into the driveway leading to Morning Glory Hill. The overhead doors, leading to the conference site, were wide open to allow the workers to move dozens of cartons inside. Stretch was surprised when he spotted a huge carnival-type gambling wheel being pushed down the ramp. It had been a long time since he had seen one like that. Hortense had asked him to help sell tickets at the back door tomorrow and he was thrilled that he would play a part in this worthwhile effort. But he was curious and he had hung around just to watch how they were going to create a casino out of empty space.

Knowing that a limited number of tickets would go on sale, Stretch bought his early. He wasn't used to spending money on his own pleasure; he chalked this expense up to his public duty. While he didn't visit casinos often, he was familiar with the wheel since it was one of the few ways to gamble that he fully understood—just choose a number, lay your money down, and hope that the damned thing stopped on the number you had chosen—much like betting on horses. He would have loved to play some of the card games, but the rules confused him. One time he had tried playing blackjack, but when he split a pair of kings when the dealer had a six showing, he was berated by the other players. Since then, he avoided the gaming tables.

Stretch was a little gun-shy when it came to gambling. It still stuck in his craw that some people thought that he had been involved in doping horses—something he never would have done—he loved the racing game too much to commit such a violation…and he loved horses even more.

Meanwhile, Harvey was standing on the stage in the main dining room, directing the men who were constructing display racks to hold some of the auction items. He wanted to make certain that the shelves were not all the same height so all kinds of prizes could be displayed for the bidders. He was amazed at the number of items that vendors had donated. It reinforced Harvey's belief that the local residents were good-hearted, generous people. Harvey was looking forward to an exciting, rewarding event. He decided that he wouldn't place any items on the shelves until later on in the evening when he had a better idea of how many things would go on the auction block. Besides, he would be able to move about more freely after the dining room had emptied out for the evening.

It was at times like these that Harvey missed being a professional event planner. This activity was extremely easy when compared to some of the huge events for which he had been responsible. He had won numerous accolades for the many conventions and conferences he had worked—getting vast spaces to look warm and friendly.

Harvey sighed and turned his attention to the cavernous space beyond the dining room, where the gaming tables would be placed. He knew that the space begged for some color, glitz, and drama. As soon as the tables had been erected, and the chairs placed around them, Harvey brought in some beautiful artificial plants. He even placed a working waterfall in one corner. He personally didn't like casinos since he felt that they were garish, noisy places, so he wanted to soften the area to make it look warmer. While he realized that this space had been developed strictly for conference exhibits, he hated the cement floor. So he needed to draw the players' eyes upwards. He purchased some netting, interspersed with little white lights. To help reduce the height of the ugly ceiling, he had the netting strung above the area over the gaming tables. As he stepped back to view the total effect, he was pleased. He hadn't lost his talent. Retirement hadn't killed his sense of what was needed to make any venue exciting. He used to worry about losing his groove—but he could cross that off his *worry list*!

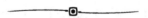

When the residents entered the dining room that evening, they saw that the curtains on the stage had been closed, and a **Do Not Enter** sign was posted on the doors leading to the conference area. Their curiosity was piqued.

"I've never seen the area behind those other doors," Marty said. "Frank, you were helping today. What does it really look like now? I hear that it's a large, barren area."

"Oh, I can't tell you that—Harvey would kill me. He was working around the clock, using his creativity everywhere. He's an amazing man," Frank said. "I think you'll be surprised at how he was able to transform that area into a casino."

"I guess I'll have to wait until tomorrow," Marty said. "I understand that with each bag of chips that we buy, we get one ticket for the drawing for three different vacation packages." Marty turned to her friends. "Wouldn't it be great if we each won one of them?" Rosebud and Ellie May nodded in agreement.

"You have to remember, Marty, there will be more outsiders at this event than residents. But, if you did win one of them, which one would you prefer?" Frank asked.

"Hmmm. That's a tough question," Marty replied.

"I would want the one for Las Vegas," Rosebud said eagerly. "I love all that glitz and glamour."

"I'd take the trip to Hawaii. I've never been there and I hear it's marvelous," Ellie May added.

"I think I would choose the cruise to the Caribbean," Marty finally said. "I've been there, but it's so fabulous that I would love to go again. I love the weather and the people are delightful. Wouldn't it be strange if it happened that way," Marty giggled, "you know, each one of us winning the trip we want? We can increase our chances of winning if we each buy two bags of chips."

Ellie May hesitated for a moment. She wasn't sure that she should spend that kind of money. "You know, I was just about to say that that idea seemed too pricey, but, Marty, you're right about increasing our chances. I didn't bat an eyelash when I spent all that money for a dress for the prom. Look at it now, hanging neatly in the back of my closet."

"But you will be able to wear that dress again," Frank reminded Ellie May.

"I'm going to wear mine tomorrow night," Rosebud said.

"Really?" Ellie May questioned.

"You bet I am. That's the sexiest dress I own."

"Hello, everyone," Fanny said amiably as she pulled out a chair to join the others at the large round table. "I'm looking forward to tomorrow night. I don't ordinarily gamble, but since this event will benefit sick children, I'm more than willing to contribute to the cause."

Just as Ellie May was about to say something, Colonel Anderson pulled out the last seat at the table and sat down. "Hello, Fanny, I'm delighted to see you again." His smile shocked everyone.

Fanny looked past him. "Frank, have the books I lent you about Abraham Lincoln been helpful in your research?"

"I surely appreciate them, Fanny. I have had a difficult time putting them aside once I started reading one of them—fascinating—simply fascinating."

"May I ask what your fascination is with Lincoln?" Anderson asked curtly.

"I'm not sure. I do remember having to give a speech on Lincoln when I was in the sixth grade. My interest in him was probably a result of my receiving an A for that talk," Frank said as he laughed.

"I certainly don't feel that Lincoln deserves all the credit he gets from historians. There are better candidates, more deserving of such honors than he was," Anderson opined. "But, if anyone says anything negative about old Abe, they're called racist. Apparently, somewhere along the line, you have been brainwashed."

"Matthew," Ellie May said sharply as she looked directly at him, "I'm so tired of your criticisms of everything and everybody. The other day you were actually mean to my grandson who had every right to talk back to you, but since he is a well-mannered child, he didn't. Then, yesterday, I was your target for an uncalled-for insult. I really don't care that my face has as many wrinkles as a well-worn map. At least my nose doesn't block out the sun. I, for one, would be happy if you would leave this table."

For a moment, everyone was quiet. All eyes were now on Anderson.

Anderson stood up. "My dear, witless woman. Just because you lack intelligence, doesn't give you the license to also demonstrate bad manners. Therefore, I will leave. Good day, all." They watched as Anderson sauntered over to an empty table and sat down.

"My goodness," Fanny said. She then looked directly at Ellie May and asked, "You were indeed rough on the poor man."

"We have had it with him," Rosebud chimed in, "he is a complete bore. You certainly cannot put the word *poor* in front of Anderson. I don't care if he does have money."

"What? Colonel Anderson is wealthy?" Fanny asked, as she looked at him with renewed interest.

"I understand that he inherited quite a large sum recently—I hear it's over seven figures. Someone in his family—I think it was an uncle—had owned oil wells or something like that," Rosebud said with a little smile on her face. "It seems that after lengthy litigation, the money was finally distributed. Maybe he'll decide to move out of here, like maybe to the Hamptons where I understand he could be with his friends the Vanderbilts. Wouldn't that be nice?"

Fanny was hanging onto every word Rosebud uttered. "I feel sorry for him," Fanny said. "I think I'll join him and see if I can cheer him up a bit."

After she knew Fanny was out of earshot, Marty said softly, "Rosebud, you made that up, didn't you?"

"Maybe yes...maybe no. Let's just see what happens to those two egomaniacs when they get together. I think they make an interesting couple. Don't you?" Rosebud said triumphantly. "You see, he has it coming."

Chapter 50

Preston was standing at the driveway directing the cars entering Morning Glory Hill for the much-anticipated casino night. Not only did he welcome everyone, he patiently gave them directions for parking, and handed them a flier explaining that an anonymous donor had pledged to match the total received from all ticket sales. Everyone was expressing their delight with the news and began to offer guesses about the identity of the donor. Preston had to admit that this assignment was fun. He usually fixed pipes, hung pictures, repaired broken appliances, and various other tasks in the apartments. Here, he was outdoors and on the fringes of all the excitement. He had never been a gambler, but he had purchased a bag of chips so his wife could have some fun bidding on the prizes. After all, it was for the kids.

Stretch felt that he had received a plum assignment. He was responsible for giving each person, who bought a bag of chips, a numbered ticket for the vacation drawings and placing the stubs in a large vat with a wooden handle. Dressed in his old jockey silks, Stretch stood on top of a wooden pallet to make himself look a bit taller. He was the talk of the crowd. It warmed his heart that so many people entering the casino remembered him from his days at the horse track.

One bearded man said, "Hey, Stretch, got any *hot* numbers for me to play on the wheel?"

"How about lucky seven?" Stretch suggested.

"Okay, I'll try that. If I hit, maybe I'll split it with you. You brought some horses in for me. Remember, TOO HOT TO HANDLE?"

"I sure do. If you win a vacation package, maybe you could take me along," Stretch kidded.

"Wait a minute. I like you, Stretch, but if I take anyone along, she will be blonde and twenty-one."

Soon there were sounds emanating from the casino that let everyone know the gaming was in full swing. People were hollering *"blackjack"* and every once in a while, someone on the crap table was rooting for a number.

Meanwhile, at the dining room door, residents of Morning Glory Hill were also checking in for a night of fun. Marty and Frank, along with Rosebud and Ellie May, were among the first to purchase their bags of chips. The Turnbulls and the Hamiltons were close behind with Nigel running to catch up with them.

"Look, Marty," Rosebud said, under her breath, "look who's coming."

Fanny had her arm linked in the colonel's and remarkably, they were both smiling.

As they approached the newly-designed casino, Frank asked, "Where would you like to begin, Marty? Would you like to try some blackjack?"

"I don't think so. You go ahead, Frank. Rosebud and I will play the big wheel awhile. We won't be hard to find. Have fun," Marty encouraged.

Climbing up on a blackjack stool alongside Gordon and Nigel, Frank said, "Mind if I join this table?"

"Welcome, Frank. You won't believe this, but my Marie is over there at the crap table. I never was a fan of that game. I used to live in Nassau and we had lots of casinos. And, although I loved table games, I didn't like the crap tables—Marie does though. If you hear her yelling, don't get too excited. That's her way of making the dice roll her way," Gordon laughed."

"Maybe I should move to the crap table and just play whatever Marie does," Nigel chuckled.

Shortly, most of the tables were filled and as soon as one player left the game, another joined the group. "Do you do this often?" Gordon asked the dealer.

"My schedule varies. I used to work at Atlantic City, but I grew tired of the rat race. I now work for *Casinos on the Go*. I work one or two nights a week," the dealer said. "This is the first time that I was in this place."

"Well, this part" said Gordon as he gestured around the room, "is used only for events such as this. The apartments here at Morning Glory

Hill are quite nice. My wife and I have been here, oh about six months or so, and we really like it. How about you, Frank, old chap?"

"I'm here a little longer than that, but I'm glad that I made the decision to live here," Frank stated while nodding his head in agreement.

Suddenly someone tapped Gordon on the back. "Gordon, old boy, just thought I'd tell you that your wife is dynamite on the crap table. She has everyone in stiches. Why, she even convinced Abigail to roll the dice. Do you believe that?" William asked.

"I surmise I'll have to take her home and lock her up," Gordon kidded.

"Oh, no, you don't," William stated firmly. "The dealers won't let you do that. See you later. I need to see how Abigail is making out."

At the end of the blackjack table. Fanny and Matthew were seated side by side. Fanny was aglow with her diamond necklace and dangling earrings. Matthew was not himself tonight—he was actually smiling. He didn't fail to notice that Fanny was leaning quite close to him.

Very quietly, Fanny whispered, "Matthew, do you know who the anonymous donor is?" She was sure that it had to be Matthew.

"I do, but I cannot tell you," he replied as he draped his arm over her chair.

"Oh, you naughty boy," Fanny cooed as she patted his leg lightly.

"Fanny, you look stunning tonight," Matthew said. "What do you gentlemen think?" he asked the other men sitting at the table.

Although they felt uncomfortable, one of them mumbled, "You're a lucky man."

"Matthew, I'm afraid I may need some help when we bid on the auction items. I am not so well-versed as you are in financial matters," Fanny said in a honeyed voice.

"My dear, you won't have to worry about finances as long as I am around, believe me," Matthew said charmingly.

Fanny whispered in Matthew's ear, "Anything you say, my Colonel, *anything*." Fanny was happier than she had been in a long time. She felt that she had hit the jackpot and, if she played her cards right, her future would no longer be in jeopardy. All she had to do to overlook his large gut and bulbous nose was to think about his fat wallet.

It was obvious that the group at the next table were enjoying themselves immensely. Harry, Harvey, and Barry had struck up a friendship with three young doctors from the hospital and the conversation was lively.

"I had never heard of Morning Glory Hill," one young intern said. "Guess I should get out and about a little more."

"I doubt that you are ready to look for independent living, young man," Barry said jokingly. "Youngsters like you might find this place just a bit boring."

"Now, just a minute, Barry. I for one disagree," Harvey said. "There's alot of fun around here. You just have to keep your ear close to the ground, so you hear all the scuttlebutt."

"What am I missing?" Barry asked.

"Why just the other day someone in the balance class had a wardrobe malfunction!"

They all laughed.

An announcement was made over the intercom to let everyone know that gambling would end in five minutes. Players were instructed to cash in their chips for play money and move to the auction area for the vacation drawings and prize bidding.

It took almost a half-hour until everyone was ready with their paper money. But, finally, the emcee asked Stretch to come up on the stage and turn the handle on the drum that held the numbered tickets. As the former jockey crossed the stage, he was met with wild applause. He once again stepped on a wooden pallet and began turning the handle.

"I understand that you recently had a prom where you chose a queen." Once again the crowd applauded. "Will Rosebud McClaren please come up on the stage and pick out the winning tickets?"

Rosebud was shocked. She was glad that she was wearing her silver gown. Stopping in front of Stretch, she asked the emcee, "What happens if I pull out my own ticket?"

The crowd roared. "Well, my dear, we may have to call in the FBI to investigate the case. But, then again, in that dress, you deserve to win."

Stretch turned the handle several times. When he stopped, the emcee opened the little door. "Your Majesty, please select a ticket."

Rosebud closed her eyes tightly. She reached down and managed to select one ticket.

The room became very quiet. "This ticket is for the cruise. It is number 6-6-8-3-7."

"No, heavens no, that's me!" said Preston's wife. She ran down the aisle, waving her ticket in the air.

When she went back to her seat, the audience applauded. She could barely see where she was going through her tears. Preston swept her off her feet and swung her around.

"Now, Your Highness, you need to draw a ticket for the Hawaii package."

All went quiet once more. Rosebud reached down, swung her hand around, and finally picked one ticket. "The winning number for the trip to Hawaii is 6-3-2-1-4. Everyone just looked around. No one was responding. "Let me repeat that. The number is 6-3-2-1-4."

"Oh, oh, that's me," said a gentleman in the back row. He walked up on the stage and talked quietly with the emcee. The emcee approached the mike. "Folks, this is a first. The gentleman who won the trip to Hawaii has decided to donate it back to the cause. So, please draw another ticket."

Once again, Rosebud drew a ticket out of the drum.

"Let's try this again. The winning number is 6-8-1-1-0."

"Whoppee, that's me," a woman near the front said.

"The last vacation prize is for Las Vegas. Once again, Your Royal Highness, select a ticket."

Rosebud followed the instructions and handed the last winning ticket to the emcee.

"The lucky number for the trip to Vegas is 6-5-6-0-3.

An elegant, older gentleman stood up. "Thank you," he said as he hurried up the aisle and onto the stage. The emcee handed the winner an envelope, which the man put in his inside jacket pocket. He then asked the emcee for the mike, and he said, "I appreciate this very much. I really love Vegas." He turned to look at Rosebud. "Perhaps I could use some company on this trip," he said as he winked at the audience who went crazy.

The gentleman took Rosebud's hand and led her down the steps. As she came down the steps, he whispered, "They think I'm kidding, but I'm not." He escorted her back to her seat. "Let me introduce myself. I am Phillip Dandridge. I would love to take you to dinner tomorrow evening so we can get better acquainted."

From that moment on, Rosebud was lost in a haze. While she heard the auctioneer as he encouraged the people to bid on the other prizes and the cheers that accompanied the awarding of each one, her mind was on Phillip.

Nigel was sitting right behind Rosebud with his arms crossed in front of him. He had heard what that stranger said to her and he was livid. He didn't know who that man was, but he hated him. How dare he embarrass Rosebud like that? He had a lot of nerve, coming in here with his fancy cuff links and Armani suit and trying to pick up Rosebud. Quietly, Nigel got up and left the room.

At the end of the auction, the emcee announced that the total amount that was raised for the hospital was $300,000. Then a huge cardboard check was carried across the stage. Pointing to the check, the emcee said, "Our unnamed donor kept his promise. Here is a check for another $300,000! Thank you all for helping us in our efforts to take care of sick children. God bless you."

"Matthew," Fanny purred, "don't you think the unnamed donor deserves a kiss?" She leaned close and kissed him deeply.

Chapter 51

It was half past five in the morning and The Square was deserted. Only Nigel and William were seated in *The Night Owl* with coffee cups in front of them.

"Who the hell did that guy think he was? He had a lot of nerve making a move on Rosebud," Nigel said angrily. "You know what I think? I think he was one of those high and mighty doctors from the hospital—that's what I think. I should have said something to him, the dirty old bastard," Nigel whined.

"Nigel," William said softly. "Let me ask you something. Do you and Rosebud have some kind of agreement or relationship...or something like that?"

"Relationship!" Nigel said, raising his voice. "Just what do you mean by that?"

"You know. Abigail and I talked that out long ago. We know where we stand with one another," William replied patiently.

"Must everything be announced nowadays? Can't you have a friendship that's just a plain old friendship?" Nigel snarled.

"Look, old buddy, Rosebud may not pay him any attention at all. And, if she does, you will have to face the facts as they are. Rosebud thinks well of you," William said as he tried to console his friend.

"Hey, I know guys like him. They dress all fancy and talk big but they are usually scoundrels at heart. Don't you think I want to protect Rosebud?" Nigel quivered.

"Certainly, but if you two have a friendship that's just a friendship, then you have no claims on the woman," William tried to explain.

"Why must everything be so complicated?" Nigel asked as he put his elbows on the table and used his hands to hold up his head. "I can't handle complications."

"Hello, gentlemen," Hortense said as she sat beside Nigel. "Are you two up early, or are you still here from last night?"

"We just arrived a bit ago," William explained.

"How did you two do at our little casino last evening?" Hortense asked.

"Nigel never left the blackjack table last night. I had a great time watching Abigail and Marie at the crap table. Gordon and I are going to take those two to Atlantic City next week," William said.

"So, Nigel, are you a blackjack expert?" Hortense inquired.

"I would rather have played poker, but they didn't offer that. I do enjoy playing blackjack, especially when the others at the table know what the hell they're doing."

Hortense laughed. "Then I won't ever sit at your table. Wasn't it nice that Preston's wife won a vacation package? Nigel, why do you look so sad?"

"I'm not sad," Nigel answered rather defensively.

"I think Nigel's experiencing a jealousy fit," William said.

"Cut that out, William," Nigel said as he stood up. "I'd like to see what you would do if some jerk made a play for Abigail. See you around," he said over his shoulder as he stomped away.

"I didn't mean to upset him," Hortense said with concern in her tone.

"Don't worry about Nigel. The problem is he and Rosebud have made several appearances demonstrating ballroom dancing. As a result, they have become good friends, but he doesn't know how to handle the off-times, if you know what I mean," William explained.

"I understand. Oh, I better be going—I'm expecting some visitors shortly. Hang around, William, one of our residents has won a prize," Hortense said mysteriously as she scurried to her office.

"Hey, Stretch, how about a refill and another doughnut," William said over his shoulder.

"Stretch left for the day, so *The Night Owl* is closed, but *Sassy's* is open," a voice from beyond the counter said.

William got up. Actually, he really wasn't interested in another doughnut. Rather, he was just trying to pass the time waiting to see what was going to happen in The Square. He grabbed a newspaper and made himself comfortable on the sofa. He felt bad about Nigel. He never would hurt Nigel's feelings...at least not intentionally. It made him feel bad to know that Nigel was upset and he hoped that the little talk he had with him helped in some way. William was reading the Opinion Page when three men came in the front door. Hortense practically fell out of her office door to greet them.

"Good morning, gentlemen, I am Hortense King, the Director of Morning Glory Hill," she said as she held out her hand.

"Miss King, it's a pleasure to meet you. I'm Ralph Werner, Editor of *Photography Today*. This is Cory Stauffer, our photographer, and this is Thomas Rider, one of the judges of our contest. As I told you on the phone, we are here to meet the winner of our 2016 contest," Werner said.

"Here he comes now," Hortense said as she spotted Harry coming across The Square with Harvey and Samuel who was carrying Oscar.

William was befuddled. He knew that Harry was a photographer, but why the strangers were making such a fuss over Oscar, he wasn't sure.

"Gentlemen," Harry said, "this is Samuel Long He was kind enough to allow Oscar to pose for me, so I owe him a debt of gratitude. And, let's not forget Oscar, who is the real winner."

"Mr. Hamilton, we would like to get some photos of this event, if you don't mind," Werner said.

"Certainly, but please include Samuel and Oscar. In fact, Mr. Werner, Samuel is such a fan of photography that I would like to recommend him for membership in our organization. How about that, Samuel?" Harry said as he wrapped his arm around the confused man.

"We'd be honored to accept Mr. Long as a member. Now, Harry, if you would stand over here please," Werner requested. He then placed the medal around Harry's neck. "And, here is your cash award," he said as he handed Harry an envelope.

"I have a gift for you, too," Mr. Rider said as he handed Harry a large framed copy of his winning photograph.

When Harry turned the photograph around, William was surprised to see Oscar lying in a bed of morning glories, looking through a pair of wire-rimmed glases. He smiled. Even William couldn't imagine a more beautiful cat in the entire world than Oscar. No wonder Harry won the prize.

"You also have the Association's permission to use this photo in any manner you choose. It is entirely your property," Mr. Werner said.

By now, a large crowd had assembled in The Square. Everyone was excited to see Oscar's photo. Samuel was beaming like a first-time father.

"Samuel, old friend," Harry said, "isn't it strange how friendships are made? One little photo, even an insignificant one, can bring people together."

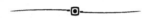

Later that night, Samuel was pacing the floor. He was trying to think things through. It appeared that Harry was planning on torturing him for a lifetime about the damned photo of him peering into the Hamilton's living room. Samuel had to make an important decision. Was he going to allow Harry to continue his diabolical plan, or should he apologize to the man?

"Oscar, Oscar, what should I do? He has me over a barrel. How can I go on like this, never knowing when Harry will show that photo to someone? But, then again, how can I allow myself to apologize to **him** of all people?"

Samuel thought of himself as a man who was adamant about his feelings for everything. After all, wasn't that his right? On one hand, he had come to like Harry—somewhat—while on the other, he still did not approve of the man's lifestyle.

"Maybe I have outlived my time, Oscar. Maybe I am too old-fashioned to fit into today's society. You, you lucky cat, don't have such problems. Perhaps the safest thing for the time being would be to forget about writing a tell-all book about the people who live at Morning Glory Hill. That's it, Oscar, I'll destroy what I have written so far and turn my attention to something else."

Samuel wiped the files from his iPad and the ones on his computer. "There, Oscar, they are gone. But, maybe not. I heard that even when you erase a file, it is still there…somewhere in that damned hard drive, waiting for someone to come along and bring it back to life. I got it. I'll get a new computer and a new iPad. And, before I take these to the recycle place, I'll mess up the hard drives. I'll whack the hell out of them. Then, I'll put them in a carton and pour molasses all over them. That should do it."

He paced some more. "I can take care of the digital evidence, but what about the photo that Harry has of me? If it ever pops up, I'll just say that I was trying to be funny. And, like most guilty people, I will deny, deny, deny."

Chapter 52

"Well, Rosebud, how did your dinner date with Phillip Dandridge go?" Marty asked eagerly.

"Let me tell you. He was everything I could hope for. His manners were impeccable, his conversations were enthralling, and I loved every minute," Rosebud said excitedly.

"Tell me more," Marty said as she curled up on her sofa.

"First of all, he's a retired surgeon and he serves on the board at the hospital. He is a widower and he has two children—a boy and a girl. And, wait till you hear this: He said that he plans on hanging onto his prize of a trip to Las Vegas until I agree to go with him! Can you imagine that?" Rosebud said like a young girl experiencing her first crush.

"Go, Rosebud, go," Marty said.

"What will people think?"

"Do you really care what they will think? You are both old enough to do as you please and if you want to go with him, go," Marty said firmly.

"I'm worried about Nigel, though. "I think he has read too much into our dancing partnership. I like Nigel, but I don't want to date him. He is really a dear, dear friend, but I have a feeling that he's a bit smitten with me," Rosebud said sadly.

"I agree with what you said, but you can't force yourself to feel differently about him, Rosebud. Have you spoken with him about your feelings?" Marty asked.

"I can't bring myself to do that," Rosebud replied. She grew quiet. "It will be painful. I guess that's why I've been putting it off. I was never good at hurting people's feelings."

"You'll find the right time, Rosebud."

"Got to run now. See you later," Rosebud said over her shoulder as she dashed out the door.

Marty was waiting for her granddaughter Laura to arrive with Gretchen. Since their return from Thailand, Marty had made it a point to be as available as possible. In the short time they had been abroad, Gretchen had grown up so fast. It seemed like only yesterday when Marty had held her and sang lullabies to her. Soon she wouldn't want to visit her great-grandmother at all. Marty vowed to treasure each moment that they had together. But, she reminded herself, she needed to make every moment meaningful—with friends, with family, and with Frank.

This was going to be a special day for Gretchen. Frank had finished the dollhouse he made for her and he was going to give it to her today. He had even bought several boxes of furniture so Gretchen could place each piece where she wanted them.

As she looked out her front window, Marty spotted Gretchen running across the lawn with a little gift bag in her hand. As Marty opened the door, Gretchen shouted, "Nana, Nana, I have a gift for you."

Gretchen wrapped her arms around Marty's legs and smiled. "It's a little doo-dad."

"Gretchen, you aren't supposed to tell what's in a gift bag," her mother said.

"I love doo-dads," Marty said as she pulled out a little ceramic figurine. "Oh, this is sweet, Gretchen. Why it's almost as pretty as you are."

"I hope you don't mind, but my errands might take a good three hours," Laura said.

"Take your time. Frank and I have plans for Gretchen today," Marty responded with a wink.

Laura kissed her daughter goodbye and reminded her to be a good girl.

"I'm always a good girl, Nana, right?" Gretchen said as she twirled around the living room floor. "Can I play with Mr. Teddy?"

"I looked for him one day, but I couldn't find him," Marty said.

"Mr. Teddy is in hyberation."

"Hyberation? What's that?" Marty asked.

"You know, Nana, you told me that bears go in hyberation and sleep all winter long. Isn't that right?" Gretchen asked. "I'll go get him."

Marty followed Gretchen into the bedroom and watched as the child lay down on the floor and reached behind the doll case.

"Here he is," Gretchen said gleefully.

Marty stared in disbelief as she saw the missing diamond necklace draped around Teddy's neck. Gretchen handed her the teddy bear and then turned her attention to the dolls. With shaking hands, Marty took the necklace off the bear's neck and slid it in her dresser drawer. She had had her friends searching for a thief who had never existed. She also realized that Rosebud and Ellie May were loyal friends. How blessed she was.

"Gretchen, we need to call Mr. Frank. He wants to come to see you today," Marty said as she picked up her cell phone. She dialed the number and then gave the phone to Gretchen. "When Mr. Frank answers, tell him we have milk and cookies for him."

When her doorbell rang, Marty could hardly contain herself. "Gretchen, let's see who's at the door."

Gretchen immediately spotted the dollhouse. She stood there quietly. Her little eyes opened wide and she put her arms around herself. "Is that for me?" she finally asked.

"You bet," Frank said as he put the dollhouse on the floor. Gretchen immediately sat down and began looking in all the windows. "And here's a bag of furniture. A little girl can't have a dollhouse without having furniture for it," Frank said.

Gretchen jumped up and gave Frank a hug. "Mr. Frank, thank you, Mr. Frank. This is the best dollhouse in the whole, whole world," she said as she began looking at the furniture.

All afternoon, the three of them played with the dollhouse, moving furniture from one room to another. It was even difficult to convince Gretchen to take a break for milk and cookies.

When Laura picked up her daughter, Marty and Frank helped to load her new gifts into the car. As they watched the car drive away, Marty said, "Frank, I hope you can stay awhile longer. I need to talk with you about something."

"I don't like the sound of that," Frank said.

Marty wasn't sure how she should begin. Frank knew nothing about the necklace. She almost felt like a criminal getting ready to confess to a horrid crime. She retrieved the necklace and laid it on a pillow on the sofa.

"Is that real?" he asked.

"I don't think so. But I'll have Rosebud examine it after I tell you the whole story."

She told Frank how she found the necklace and why it had bothered her so much. Then she explained that before she had had a chance to have her friends examine it, the necklace disappeared. The bulk of her story was about the fiasco that followed, as the three of them tried to find out who took the necklace.

Frank's mouth was hanging open. "I love it...I wish we would have a video of how the three of you conducted an investigation... pawn shops...*Serenity*...the food bank and all of that," Frank laughed heartily. "Marty, you have the necklace now, so call Rosebud and ask her to come here."

"I also need to call Ellie May. She'll want to hear about this, too," Marty said as she turned to her phone once again.

When everyone was there, Rosebud picked up the necklace. "I could use my jewelers loupe, but I don't think I need it. These are not real diamonds. However, they are very well made and the piece could bring in more than a thousand dollars."

"What a bummer," Ellie May said sadly. "Thinking they were real diamonds has been such fun for us."

"Marty, do you want to sell the necklace?" Frank asked.

"I don't think so. But I would like to put it to good use somehow," Marty said.

"Okay, then, I have an idea. We're going to the mall," Frank said.

"The mall?" Ellie May said. "Why the mall?"

"Are you all in agreement that you want this necklace to bring some good to someone?" he asked. Hearing no objections, Frank said, "Okay then, let's go. It will become clear once we get there."

As Frank pulled his car into the parking lot, Marty said, "I wonder if there's a problem inside. I see two fire trucks."

"The firemen are collecting for their annual Thanksgiving food drive for the food bank. At each of the doorways. you'll see firemen holding large rubber boots to collect donations. We're going to donate this necklace."

For a moment, there was dead silence inside the car. "Frank, that's an absolutely fabulous idea. You couldn't have chosen a better way to get rid of the necklace," Marty said as she leaned over and kissed him on his cheek.

"I have wrapped the necklace in a large handkerchief. Marty, casually drop this and we'll all follow putting money in the boot. Relax and don't bring any attention to us. That way the donation will be anonymous," Frank explained.

"This is so thrilling," Ellie May said. "Of all the scenarios that I thought up about the necklace, this is so much better."

"We need to keep this between the four of us. I'm certain that the firemen will either put it up for auction or sell it some way. It will be fun to be the only ones who know the truth," Frank said. "Okay, ladies, let's go shopping."

The four walked across the parking lot. Marty's heart was pounding. She had wanted to do something more for the food bank, and Frank's idea was perfect. As they approached the doorway, they were surprised to see that it was Preston who was holding the fireman's boot. As Marty dropped the little package into the boot, her hands were shaking. Rosebud was making a fuss about the size of the large yellow boot and was making Preston laugh. One by one, they dropped in their donations.

Chapter 53

Everyone at Morning Glory Hill was still talking about the necklace that the firefighters found in one of their boots they used to collect donations for the food bank last weekend. The local newspaper had a picture of Preston on their front page, holding the unique piece of jewelry. While a local jeweler quickly informed them that the stones in the piece were not real, he had indicated that it was still a beautiful necklace and had recommended that the food bank put it up for auction.

Those interested in the piece had to submit a sealed bid by noon today. *The Happy Four,* as they had nicknamed themselves, were seated in front of Marty's TV to watch the opening of the bids on a local, cable station.

"I can't believe that they only received six bids," Ellie May said.

"You have to remember, Ellie May, that the necklace was a bit gaudy for most people," Rosebud said. "There probably would have been more bids if the required opening bid had not been set at $1,000."

"Frank offered to place a bid for me if I wanted the necklace back," Marty said.

"Yeah, and she almost bit my head off when I said that," Frank said as he laughed.

"Well, it gave me more problems than it was worth," Marty said. "I was relieved to get it out of my apartment and out of my mind."

To add to the excitement of the auction, Mayor Peguese had agreed to open the bids and announce the offers.

"As agreed upon, the mayor said, I will announce the amount of the bid, but not the name of the bidder." He then took the first envelope in his hand and said, "This bid is for $1,500...the next one is for $1,200... the third is $1,800...the fourth is $1,500...the fifth is $1,900...and the last is for $2,500. Since this bidder is from out-of-town, he will be notified and arrangements will be made for him to pick up the necklace. Ladies and gentlemen, thank you for your bids, and I am pleased to announce that the total amount of money that the firemen have raised this drive for the food bank has just gone over the $8,000 mark. Congratulations!"

After Frank turned the TV off, Marty said, "You know what I think? I think that it was Veronica Martindale who made the final bid for the necklace. I honestly think that that was the reason she visited me. She probably wanted to be certain that no one else would be able to connect it with the one that was stolen as she had claimed."

"What makes you think that?" asked Rosebud.

"Looking back on her visit to me, I think she wanted the paste version of the real necklace that was supposedly stolen from their safe. I think that they got away with an insurance scam," Marty said convincingly.

"Does that mean we can begin another investigation?" Ellie May asked excitedly as she moved forward in her chair.

"Heavens, no. If it were a scam, we could run into a hornet's nest if we do that," Marty said. "We need some peace and quiet around here."

"But, Marty, it would be so much fun. Listen, I watched a show that came close to this scam and we could become heroes!" Ellie May said. "We might even earn a reward from the insurance company."

"Ladies, that could be very dangerous," Frank said cautiously.

Ellie May pursued her lips together. "You know, Frank, you may be right. I wouldn't want anything to happen to anyone of us over a piece of jewelry."

Marty said, "Let's drink a toast to celebrate our ridiculous venture into the investigation business. Frank, please pour the wine."

As *The Happy Four* held their glasses high, Marty said, "I don't think there ever will be a foursome like us. Think of it, guys. We had fun looking for a necklace that wasn't even missing…we investigated people who never knew that we had them on our suspects' list…and a lot of money was raised for a good cause. Frank, we thank you for coming up with a solution to our quagmire."

Ellie May was lost in thought. She didn't want the fun to stop. Perhaps if she waited a couple of days, she might be able to talk them into investigating the insurance scam. *That* would really be exciting!

Chapter 54

Celeste was just coming out the front door of Morning Glory Hill when Ernesto, her favorite van driver, pulled up to the curb. As she climbed the three steps to get into the van, she asked, "Have you heard the news?"

"Yes, unfortunately, I did," Ernest said sadly. "It sure is hard to accept, isn't it?"

"I was shocked to learn who it was. Of all the people who live here, I wasn't ready to see one of my best library patrons be the first to go." Celeste said with a quiver in her voice.

"Celeste, I must run in and check with Mary Beth. I thought she told me that I would have two passengers this morning. I don't want to leave anyone behind. I'll be right back. You won't be late for your appointment at The Health Center," Ernesto reassured Celeste.

Just then the hearse began to move. As it neared the van, Celeste put her hand up against the glass window and whispered one of her favorite sayings: *Never shall I forget the days which I spent with you.* While Ludwig van Beethoven had said this many years ago, the words somehow brought her comfort, like a warm blanket on a wintery night. As the hearse drove past her window, Celeste felt a sensation in her hand—one that seemed to say, *I know, my friend.*

Ernesto returned to the van. He realized by her body language that Celeste was thinking about the friend she had just lost. They rode in silence to The Health Center. Ernesto knew that sometimes silence is better than the most eloquent soliloquy ever spoken.

Printed in the United States
By Bookmasters